CW00859609

1 MONTH OF
FREE
READING

at

www.ForgottenBooks.com

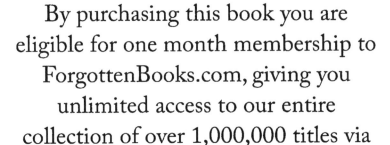

By purchasing this book you are eligible for one month membership to ForgottenBooks.com, giving you unlimited access to our entire collection of over 1,000,000 titles via our web site and mobile apps.

To claim your free month visit:

www.forgottenbooks.com/free214211

* Offer is valid for 45 days from date of purchase. Terms and conditions apply.

ISBN 978-0-483-54807-7
PIBN 10214211

This book is a reproduction of an important historical work. Forgotten Books uses state-of-the-art technology to digitally reconstruct the work, preserving the original format whilst repairing imperfections present in the aged copy. In rare cases, an imperfection in the original, such as a blemish or missing page, may be replicated in our edition. We do, however, repair the vast majority of imperfections successfully; any imperfections that remain are intentionally left to preserve the state of such historical works.

Forgotten Books is a registered trademark of FB &c Ltd.
Copyright © 2018 FB &c Ltd.
FB &c Ltd, Dalton House, 60 Windsor Avenue, London, SW19 2RR.
Company number 08720141. Registered in England and Wales.

For support please visit www.forgottenbooks.com

WE BOYS.

Written by One of Us for the Amusement of Pa's and Ma's in General, Aunt Lovisa in Particular.

BOSTON:
ROBERTS BROTHERS.
1876.

COPYRIGHT, 1876.
BY ROBERTS BROTHERS.

Stereotyped and Printed by
ALFRED MUDGE & SON

CONTENTS.

We Boys.

AUTHOR'S NOTE.

June 15, 18—.

I, Bob Brown, begin this writing on a lot of bluish paper I've found in the lower drawer of the secretary, and that mother says I may have for my own.

WE BOYS.

"WILL BRADLEY AND I."

CHAPTER I.

INTRODUCES TWO OF US BOYS.

WILL BRADLEY and I live in Baywater, State of Massachusetts. We belong to that portion of the inhabitants called "small boys," but we always go to town-meeting and hurrah for the man who 's elected just as if we 'd voted for him. Will says that's one of the advantages of not being of age. After we 're twenty-one we can't shout unless our man 's elected; now we are sure of the shouting anyway. Will's father is a democrat, and believes the republicans are ruining the country, but Will hurrahs for the republicans until he's purple in the face. My father is a republican, and believes the democrats would bring disgrace and ruin upon the nation, but I 've scraped the skin off my throat time and again yelling for a democrat.

Will and I are those two boys who, a good deal of the time, stand on the porch or around the hitching-posts in front of Bradley & Co.'s store. We are blowing into the horses' nostrils, or watching for something to come up the street. When a man of about our size appears we hail him with the inquiry whether he has any marbles about him; provided he has, and his mother is n't in a hurry about his bringing home the sugar, we 're the two boys who, with a third boy and one other, are playing marbles in the rear of the horse-sheds.

Will's father is in the dry-goods and grocery business, and Will says if there's anything he hates it is dry-goods and groceries. My father is cashier of the Baywater Bank, and I do think a cashier's is the stupidest business!

Will and I go to the same school. We've always been to the same school and been in the same class since we learned to spell "a man," "a boy," "a girl" in Hillard's First Primary. Will hasn't been a much better scholar than I am. I heard his mother and mine talking about it once. My mother said that arithmetic seemed to come hard to me, and Will's mother said so it did to Will. Will's mother said that he didn't take to geography naturally, and my mother said no more did I. Then both our mothers said we didn't appear to have much taste for grammar; grammar was so dry they said they didn't wonder. My mother said she didn't believe in boys studying too hard, it undermined the constitution. Will's mother said she thought there was danger of weak eyes from it.

I told Will, and we both agreed with our

mothers. "Let's draw it easy, Bob!" said Will, and then we both fell a-giggling.

We sit together in school, and Will is a capital fellow to sit beside. He can make the nicest kind of paper wheels to buzz around on a pin, and can draw old women in ruffled night-caps. He always has something interesting in his pockets, — windmills, dancing cork-figures, strips of elastic tape, grasshoppers tied together with a thread, or bumble-bees shut up in a tin box.

Out of a piece of wood and a bit of hoop-skirt steel he contrived a kind of spring-gun with which we can shoot off peas and beans. We each of us have one.

One day when Almira Harris and the master were explaining algebra at the blackboard, Will aimed a bean at Almira's back-hair, but it missed, and went plump against the black-board. The master turned around. Will's hand was raised, and his forehead knotted up in wrinkles; he was trying to find "what three large rivers flow into the Bay of Bengal."

The master boxed Tommy Taylor on one ear

for snapping off the bean, and on the other ear for starting to say he did n't snap it; boxed me on both ears for laughing; and told Will that the three rivers were the Ganges, Brahmapootra, and Irrawaddy. Then he turned back to the blackboard and to Almira, and Will fired at Susanna Anastasia Vallandigham, — we call her Sue, for short, — and hit her on the cheek. Sue put up her hand, and said she, "Someun 's snapping beans."

The master turned around in his sternest way. "Who dare shoot beans again?" asked he.

We all looked around to see who it was. Tommy Taylor had his head down on the desk crying, so we knew it could n't be he. I looked hard at Cynthia Strong, as if I strongly suspected it was she, and Will put his finger on the map of China, so as not to lose the place, and looked at her as if he had n't any doubts but that it was she. Cynthia is surly and a tell-tale, and we boys detest her, but I don't think we did quite right there.

No one told who it was, and after Will had said he did n't remember the name of the second river that flowed into the Bay of Bengal, and the master had said "Brahmapootra," he turned to the blackboard again. By and by Will fired another bean at the master's back. It hit him fairly between the shoulders; but Almira was crying then because she didn't understand radical signs, the master was trying to comfort her, and never knew that he was a dead man.

Oh! Will is a jolly boy, and he and I are the best of friends. I am going to write about some of the things we do.

CHAPTER II.

A BITTER WEDNESDAY.

ONE out of every two Wednesdays the girls in our school read compositions and the boys declaim. Our class have n't, until this term, had a part in these exercises, but after the master had dismissed school the day Will and I had such good luck in shooting, he called our class up to his desk, and told us that he expected us to take part in the exercises the next Wednesday.

We all shrugged our shoulders and some of us said, "Oh gracious!" Nellie Royce and Rose Payson began to cry and to say they could n't write a composition, and could n't read it if they wrote one. Sue Vallandigham went after her shawl, muttering that she would n't come on Wednesday.

"Oh, yes you will, Sue," said Homer Sharpe; "you always bluster badly in the beginning, but in the end you do just as the other girls do."

Sue flirted her shawl-fringe in his face, and said she would like to know what boys were made for.

"Made to be a comfort to girls in times of affliction," said Homer.

Cynthia Strong, who was just behind Sue, and who always has to put in her word, said they were nothing but a torment.

"Miss Strong," said Homer, falling back with Cynthia, "if it'll relieve your feelings I'll write your composition for you."

Cynthia scorned to reply, except by elevating her pugnacious little nose.

Will had heard his father tell about speaking the "Battle of Hohenlinden" when he was a boy, and Will thought he should like that. I went over to Mr. Bradley's that evening, and we hunted up an old reading-book, and found the poem. On the opposite page was one that Will thought would be the thing for me. It was about Marco Bozzaris. I wonder who he was, anyway. It was too long for me, but

Will said the first two verses would be a great plenty, and I thought, myself, it would be quite as impressive to finish off with,—

> "Strike—for your altars and your fires!
> *Strike*—for the green graves of your sires,
> God and your native land!"

When I told my mother about it, she said that was n't suitable for me, and wished me to learn something out of a gilt-edged book of hers, but that was so tame I plead off.

After the classes had read Wednesday afternoon, the master called the large girls out to read compositions, and after those, the girls in our class. First came Rose Payson and Nellie Royce; but Rose read so low and so fast we could n't understand her, and Nellie's voice trembled so much we did n't like to look at her.

Hattie Davis and Molly Hammond came next, and after them, Cynthia Strong and Sue Vallandigham.

Cynthia walked on to the platform, with a little flirt to her clothes, and began reading before Sue was hardly in position. Will and I committed her composition to memory, and now, when she 's particularly obstreperous, we say it over to her: —

FLOWERS.

"Who does not love flowers? There are many kinds of flowers. I will mention some of them: petunias, marigolds, holly hocks, roses, and sweet peas. There is also larkspur, verbenas, and oleanders. Trailing arbutus grows wild. So no more for this time."

The title of Sue's composition was "Self-Education." It was largely moral.

She said that self-education was the best kind of education, and that if we did n't get an education while we 're young, we should n't have one when we grew older. She said we ought to study and improve our time in school, and not be drawing pictures on our slates nor playing tit, tat, too (there is n't a scholar in school who plays tit, tat, too, as much as Sue does); and then she said we should be prepared to fight the battles of life. Almost all the men we read about in books were self-educated men.

George Washington, Daniel Webster, Alexander the Great, Nero, Cicero, and Benjamin Franklin were all self-educated men, and so might we be if we would only try, and we should be glad of it all our lives. She hoped we should all make up our minds to be self-educated men, and come to school steady, not be tardy, but try to please our teacher, and so make useful, self-educated men.

When she finished, the master said there were some errors in her enumeration of self-educated men; but I did n't understand what they were, for Will had his hands under the desk just then, making deaf-and-dumb letters to me.

The master said we would listen to the declamations.

We have some powerful speakers in our school. I 've heard Wendell Phillips and I 've heard Mr. Gough, but neither of them can stir me up as Gustus Hillman or Isaac Tucker can.

Gustus' declamation this afternoon was the speech of a Thracian gladiator. Gustus has a round, fat face and a snubby nose, but he has a powerful voice, and makes a tremendous gladiator. He aroused my sympathy in the very beginning, and when he told how the Romans butchered his brother, "a beautiful youth, scarce seventeen summers old," I felt as if I wanted to run them through with my dagger; when he told how fierce and mad with blood he had become, and how many Romans he had slain, I did n't blame him at all; but when he raised his hands and eyes to the heavens, and appealed to the gods above to hear him, my heart fairly stood still.

When he made his final bow to the school, and returned through the aisle, past my seat, I felt terribly depressed and discouraged about my "piece." It seemed as if anything I could do would be miserably poor in comparison with this.

Ike immediately took the floor. Ike is a rather thin, long-legged fellow, not very handsome, but I call him a splendid speaker. He has such long arms he can make splendid gestures. When he made his bow he scraped back his foot with considerable noise, then in a loud voice announced, —

THE TAKING OF WARSAW.

"When leagued oppression poured to Northern wars
Her whiskered pandoors and her fierce hussars,
Waved her dread standard in the breeze of morn,
Pealed her loud drum and twanged her trumpet-horn,
Tumultuous horror brooded o'er the van,
Presaging wrath to Poland — and to man!"

I can't repeat any further, but I know that at one time Ike waved his arm on high and begged his fellow-men to rise, and swear for the country to live or with her to die. I, for one, would have rose in a minute if the other boys would. When he hissed out, "Revenge or death the watch-word and reply," I grasped my spring-gun; but when "Freedom shrieked and Kosciusko fell," I thought my hair would stand up straight. Then he sunk his voice to a low tone, and told how the sun went down, and the battle went on, and there was fire and blood-dyed water and storm, shaking of the earth, and a thousand hopeless shrieks for mercy, —

"——— red meteors flashed along the sky,
And conscious Nature shuddered at the cry."

Ike wound up, calling loudly for "the patriot Tell and Bruce of Bannockburn." Those gentlemen, had they come, would probably have set things right again.

After Ike came the other large boys, and then we small boys. Charlie Payson spoke "A Child's Address to a Star." It was n't "Twinkle, twinkle," but it was about as childish. Homer Sharpe had something from a newspaper. It was funny and made the scholars laugh, but Will wrote on the slate that it was n't *classical*, like mine and his.

Will was called directly after Homer. He had n't studied his "piece" hardly at all, and I was so afraid he could n't say it that my cheeks flamed up and my knees shook. Will is one of those boys, though, who think they can go through anything, and he marched out and took the floor just as Ike had done. He made a very low bow, and in a sepulchral voice began, —

"On Linden, when the sun was low,
All bloodless lay the untrodden snow,
And dark as midnight was the flow
Of Iser rolling rapidly.

"But Linden saw another sight
When the drums beat at dead of night,"

"When the drums beat at dead of night—" He could n't go any further. The master prompted; Will repeated, and again he came to a dead stop. The master prompted again; Will said a few words more, could n't think, skipped three or four lines, and then struck in strongly.

Just as the Iser was rolling rapidly the second time I put my hand in my pocket for my handkerchief and hit my spring-gun. It struck me that it would be a good joke to just pop a bean into Will's face. So I pulled out the gun, loaded her up, and fired. The charge took him right in the eye. He jumped, and the bean went rattling off on the floor.

"Pause for a moment, Bradley," said the master, looking over the scholars.

"'Twas him, sir," said Cynthia Strong, pointing her stubby fore-finger at me.

The blood bounded into my face, and the pupils of my eyes must have grown large.

"Robert Brown, were you discharging projectiles across the school-room, sir?"

"Were I what, sir?"

"Were you firing beans, sir?"

I dropped my head, and whispered, "Yes, sir."

"You may stand in your seat. I will attend to your case very shortly, sir."

I didn't pay any further attention to Will, but I knew when he was through, for the master said, "Young Brown may walk this way."

I walked out towards the master's desk.

"You may step upon the platform, face the school, and apologize for disorderly conduct," said he.

I stepped up to the place he indicated. All the large boys and small boys, all the big girls and little girls, were looking at me. The room was so still you could have heard a pin drop. It seemed as if the floor was sinking underneath me, and yet I could n't go out of sight. Oh, dear, *dear!* how I wished I'd never shot off that bean! I wished I 'd never seen a bean, never seen a spring-gun either. My heart was up in my mouth, my throat was dry, I could n't speak.

"Quick!" said the master.

"Please excuse me —" gasped I.

"For disorderly conduct," said the master.

"For disorderly conduct," repeated I.

"Very well, sir," said he, "don't let such a misdemeanor occur again. You may stand a little farther down this way, and we will listen to your declamation."

I knew my declamation was about Marco Bozzaris, and that was all I did know about it.

I made my bow, and said,—

"Marco Bozzaris."

I had been repeating the lines over to myself all the afternoon, but now I could n't think of one word of them. Will had the book, and commenced for me: —

> "At midnight, in his guarded tent."

> "At midnight, in his guarded tent,"

said I.

> "The Turk was dreaming of the hour,"

put in Will.

> "The Turk was dreaming of the hour,"

repeated I.

"When Greece, her knee in suppliance bent,
Should tremble at his power,"

said Will.

"When Greece, her knee in suppliance bent,
Should tremble at his power,"

said I.

Will supposed that after that start I should be able to go on; but I was n't. I tried to remember what came next, but I could n't. I could n't think of anything but just "The frog he would a-wooing go, a-wooing go, 't rinktum, rinktum, botti-metti kimo." That ran through my head over and over again.

It seemed as if the blood would burst through my face. Will, I knew, was distressed. Some of the girls began to titter.

"You may have your seat, Rob," said the master.

I went to my seat, put my head down upon my desk, and did n't look up until after school was out. Will kept nudging me and nudging me.

As soon as school was dismissed, the boys, large and small, came flocking around me.

"Never mind, Bob," said Ed. Hammond, "you'll do better next time."

"Yes, Bob," said Ike, "and you took your sentence like a little hero."

"You're a regular little Roman, Bob; and if some one'll write a poem about you, Ike and I will do you justice in the oratorical line," said Gustus.

Will had my hand in his, squeezing it.

"Come, Bobberty," said he, "you and I must 'strike for our homes, our altars, and our fires.'"

I wiped my eyes and lifted up my head.

All the large boys bade me good-by, and filed out. Charlie Payson brought my cap, and slapped it on my head, and we started off.

When I reached home, mother, with my little brother Freddy, had gone out making calls, and Aunt Lovisa was running the sewing machine; so there was no one to ask me any questions.

I was afraid mother would hear about my having been "called up" in school, or that some one would tell my father, and I knew they would be terribly ashamed of me. But when they came home, they did n't appear to know anything about it, nor did my father ask me, as he sometimes does, how school went. I was very glad of that.

CHAPTER III.

A SWEET SATURDAY.

SATURDAY morning my mother wanted to make some gingerbread, and as the molasses was all gone, she sent me down to Mr. Bradley's store for some more.

Frank Simmons, the clerk, had just knocked out the head of a hogshead from which the molasses had been drawn off, and Will was down on his knees before it, eating out the soft sugar with his fingers. He said that his father had given him the sugar, and he was going to melt it into syrup, and sell it back to him.

"Run home with your jug, Bobberty, and then come back and help me," said he.

I ran home so fast that the molasses slopped up and down, and out around the cork of my jug. Mother gave me permission to return.

"I should not think you would allow it, Almira. He and that Bradley boy run the streets altogether too much already," said my Aunt Lovisa.

"He is n't going to run the streets, Lovisa," replied my mother.

I wish Aunt Lovisa would n't meddle with my affairs quite so much as she does; she is n't my mother nor my father either.

When I got back to the store Will had taken out two pailfuls of sugar, and was in the hogshead still scraping. He invited me in, but said I must be careful about sitting down.

When we went up to the house with the sugar, and Will told his mother he was going to melt it over, she scowled, but on looking at him, she began laughing.

"Are you going to boil yourself up?"

"No, I'm not. But you just help us a little, — get us going straight, you know, won't you?"

She said she supposed she should, but she had better send for Mrs. Donovan to follow us up with the scrubbing cloth. Will promised to be very, *very* careful.

"Yes, I know; boys always are careful," said she.

She put the sugar melting, cautioned us against coming into the sitting-room, because we should stick to everything there, and went off.

We stuffed the wood into the stove, and the room grew so hot and steamy that we could hardly breathe. Will thrust his head into the sitting-room, and begged to go in there; but his mother said, no, we must stay and watch our syrup; it was liable to run over.

It did n't look much like running over; it was n't half-way up to the top of the kettle.

"Run over? No!" said Will. "I 'm more afraid you and I shall run down. I feel like a tallow candle set in an oven. Just throw up that north window, will you?"

We sat down by the window and began playing backgammon. As soon as we were fairly playing, the sirup began to sizzle over. Will flew at it, and dropped in a chunk of butter to break the bubbles. Then he seized the stove-hook and tried to poke off the sugar that was boiling and smoking on the stove. He daubed it all over the hook, all over his hands, and got a little on his face.

"Oh, dear, Bob!" exclaimed he, throwing down the hook and blowing his burnt hands. "I wish the stuff was all in 'Greenland's icy mountains'!"

So did I. The room was blue with smoke, and more smoke was all the time rising from the stove.

Will brought from the wood-shed one of his mother's scrubbing cloths, and tried wiping off the syrup with that. He burnt his fingers, and then I tried, and burnt my fingers. The rag was tender, and pieces of it stuck to the stove. We both stepped in the sugar that had drizzled on to the floor, and tracked that out into the wood-shed. Just then the door opened, and Will's mother came out.

"O *boys!*" exclaimed she.

"I did n't expect it was going to act like this, mother," said Will, fingering his burns and not looking up.

"I suppose you did n't expect it," said she, fixing her eyes on the backgammon board.

"Well, you see, mother — " began Will.

"Yes, I see," said she.

Will put his fingers to his mouth, and blew on them fiercely. His mother stood and looked at him. I felt as if I should like to run out at the back door, and home.

After it all, Will had the boldness to ask her if he might invite two or three boys, and have a candy pull in the afternoon. She talked to him a while because he had been so careless, then gave the permission, and we left to look up the boys.

We came upon Homer in the street. Mr. Sharpe owns a tin-shop, and Homer, when he is n't in school, is errand-boy. He was carrying a gridiron and a dozen tin pans up to Deacon Clapp's. He said he would come.

We went on to Charlie Payson's. Mr. Payson is wealthy, and keeps a gardener and a groom, and Charlie don't need to work at all unless he chooses, but he is always busy. We found him in the carriage-house, with his carpenter's tools, making the side-pieces for a wheelbarrow.

Mike Flaherty, the gardener, who lay stretched out on the floor, said Charlie 'd paid out two months' allowance for that old "whalebarrow" frame.

"And it's joost good for clutter," said he.

"Now, Mike, what's the use of telling that? You said yourself that the wheel was good, and the frame stout; you know you did."

"Boot what nade have we of it? We've a whalebarrow as good as new alriddy"

Charlie said he expected to run this one himself. When he finished it we should see what we should see. He was as ready to accept Will's invitation as Homer had been, and we went home.

We met at Mr. Bradley's at two o'clock. Will had put the syrup on in his mother's jelly-kettle. She said he had twice as much as he needed, and a third more than he could boil down, and he was dipping it out with a teacup.

After the syrup was set over the fire we kept a close watch over it, and we each of us had a spoon with which to try it, — each of us but Will; he had a little wooden paddle that he had whittled out and that he greatly delighted in. We kept tasting and tasting, burning our tongues and burning our tongues.

We had only just begun working the candy

when the cat jumped upon the table and began smelling the butter. Then Homer's shoe-strings came untied and Charlie's hair kept falling over his eyes; the flies troubled us and some one knocked at the back door.

Homer said he wished he had something with which to flavor his candy, and Will scrambled up on the table, and took from the little cupboard over it a greenish glass bottle. He pulled out the cork, and smelled it.

"Hold your hands, Home," said he.

Homer put his hands together, and Will poured into them a spoonful of camphor.

"Cracky!" cried Homer.

"Why, it's camphor, is n't it?" said Will, holding the bottle to his nose, and making up a dreadful face.

"Here's all sorts of flavoring extracts up here, Home," said Will, his head still in the cupboard. "Here's picra — good for worms. Have some of this?" said he, shaking a vial of nasty-looking black stuff over Homer's head.

"Get down, Will!" said Charlie. "Home has flavoring enough for this time."

"Oh! I can dispose of this easily enough. Women like camphor; it's good for faintness. I'll make this up for the lady of my heart, — the angelic Cynthia."

"Have a little cayenne in it then, won't you?" asked Will, who still stood upon the table.

He reached down a little package of red pepper, and Homer turned as much into his candy as it would hold.

"O Homer!" said Charlie, "what a mess you are going to have!"

"What a mess Cynthia is going to have, you mean. Serve her right; she blabbed on Bob the other day."

"It won't hurt her," said Will, sitting down on the edge of the table and swinging his legs. "Cayenne's irritating, but camphor's healing."

Homer shaped the candy into a short, clubby kind of a stick and laid it on the platter. I had just put down mine; mine was quite white, and twisted into little sticks about three inches long.

"O Bob!" said Homer, "what *are* you going to do with those lily-fingers all laid in a row?"

I said I should give them to my Aunt Lovisa. Then I felt my cheeks and forehead flush up. I did n't intend to tell a fib about it, but I had thought of Nellie Royce.

Charlie said he thought he should make a man, and we all began making men. Charlie's was a very fine one, but Homer's was n't so natural. He rolled up one large ball for the body, then one smaller ball for the head. The head was half as large as the body and the shape of a fly's head. One leg was larger round at the ankle than at the thigh, and the other was too short.

Will made a girl. He tried to make her waist waspy and fashionable, but the skirt would n't hang to it; so he made it broad, and said she was a good, sensible girl who did n't lace. He gave her a small head, but a good stout neck, for he said he wanted her to hang together if she did n't do anything else. He stuck a couple of feathers on her head for hair, and pushed two bits of charcoal into her face for eyes. He named her Susanna Cynthia Angelina Bradley.

"Call her 'Glina for short, boys," said he.

I did n't have very good luck with my man, so I just made him over into sticks. The rest of the candy we worked into rings, crosses, and balls.

Charlie said he wished we could wipe up the molasses we had drizzled about, and Will said he wished so, too, for it had taken his mother an hour to clean up the room in the morning. So he brought the dishcloth and another rag, and we rolled up our sleeves and we washed the kettle, the pan, the plates, and all the spoons; we rubbed off the table, the stove, and all the chairs, and Homer mopped the floor.

We helped Will carry his molasses down to the store. There was between six and seven gallons of it, and Mr. Bradley paid him fifty cents a gallon. Will wanted to buy some almonds and "treat"; but his father said he had done treating enough for one day; it was time we scattered. Mr. Bradley had neuralgia in the face, and we did scatter.

When I got home I offered Aunt Lovisa some

candy. She asked if Mrs. Bradley or we made it. I told her we did, all ourselves; and she said she thanked me, she would'n't take any. Mother ate two sticks, and said it was very nice indeed.

CHAPTER IV.

A SCHOOL DAY WITH US BOYS.

WHEN I went down to school Monday morning, Will was out in front of the store helping pack away bundles and bags under the seat of Capt. Parker's old buggy. There was a bushel of hay-seed in a bag, a pailful of oats in which the captain had brought eggs to market, a bag of fine salt, and a half-bushel of coarse salt. The captain stumped back into the store, and Will called my attention to the things.

"This bundle holds candles," said he, thrusting a brown-paper parcel under my nose. "And here 's half a pound of tea. The captain's geography is rather confused. He wanted Japanese, and he called for Egyptian. He said he 'd take 'second best,' 'cause he did n't drink tea himself, but his 'old woman' had to have her brew three times a day. He 's got a dress for the 'old woman' in this bundle. I just wish you could see it. I don't know where this molasses jug is going. Stand out of the way now; the captain's flour-barrel is coming."

Frank rolled out the barrel, and he and the captain loaded it into the wagon. Then the captain climbed in, and said, "Gad up!" The old wall-eyed, bob-tailed mare gave a kind of a spring and a jump, and started off with a great clattering of loose machinery about the wagon, while the ends of the colt-skin robe swung to and fro over the back of the seat.

"Is n't it wonderful that the old rack-o'-bones mare can travel so?" said Will, as we started towards the school-house.

"Yes; and it seems to me more wonderful that the old wagon don't go to pieces," said I.

"Kind of all go down together, like 'the deacon's one-hoss shay'? *Squatulate*, you mean, don't you?"

"Yes, *squatulate*."

Just then Homer came running from the school-house towards us. Homer has a peculiar, jerky kind of a gait, and when he runs, he runs all over, his elbows flying back and forth as rapidly as his legs.

"Hullo!" said he.

"Hullo!" responded we.

"The fair Cynthia has arrived," shouted he. "I 've been waiting for you before making the presentation."

Will came to a sudden stop. "There, now, I 've left my girl at the store! Wait a minute, boys, and I 'll run back and get her."

Homer and I waited in the yard until Will came back; then we all went into the school-house. Cynthia stood with two or three other girls on the "girls' side," and Homer walked up and held out to her the cayenne-camphor candy.

"Miss Strong," said he, "will you please accept the contents of this parcel as a trifling token of the high esteem I feel for you?"

"Who made it?" asked Cynthia.

"I did, my angel."

"I 'd sooner eat *pizen!*" said Cynthia, and she sent the candy whizzing over to the other side of the school-room.

"I also have brought an offering," said Will, taking out of his pocket his girl, which was linty, and looked worse, if anything, than it did Saturday.

"I don't wish for it, thank you; it resembles the artist too closely," said Cynthia, tartly.

Will sold it to little Tommy Taylor for two slate pencils.

I waited by the entry door, and when Nellie came, I slipped into her hand the candy I had saved for her. She thanked me quick and low, and tucked it into her pocket. Homer saw her eating it, and asked me if she was my Aunt Lovisa, and he and Will called her Aunt Lovisa all the rest of the day.

The candy that Cynthia threw away fell in Ike Tucker's seat, and some of the boys laid it on his desk. Ike did n't come in until nearly ten o'clock. He supposed some friend had put the candy there for him, ducked his head under the desk and took a good big bite. Just then his geometry class was called.

He was under the desk, coughing, spitting, and sputtering at a great rate.

"Don't keep the class waiting, Tucker," said the master.

Ike swallowed the candy and came out looking like a picture in Fox's "Book of Martyrs."

I held my nose, but it was n't of any use, I snickered out; so did Will and Homer. We got five marks apiece for it, and in two or three minutes Will burst out again, — just like a bladder that pops because it 's too full. He got five more for that.

About a half an hour afterwards, Tommy Taylor was fumbling around under his desk, and he pushed Will's girl out slap into the aisle. She was so soft that she didn't break, but the master saw and confiscated her.

Just before afternoon session opened, Cynthia came out with a very remarkable story about the way we had cleaned up Mrs. Bradley's kitchen. Will fired up and denied much of it, and he and Cynthia had a regular up-and-down, out and-out dispute over it; and after the bell rang Will took out his slate and drew a female portrait, supposed to represent Cynthia. Tommy Taylor saw it, and held up his hand to tell. Will made savage motions at him; but he only run his hand up higher, and I think he would have told, but just then the committee and the committee's son walked in.

The committee is Mr. Anson Pomeroy. The committee's son is Daniel Webster Pomeroy. He belongs to a college.

Just before school closed, Mr. Pomeroy took the register out of the desk to examine, and found Will's girl stuck on the back side of it. The expression of his face, as he peeled her off, was too jolly. He could n't have been more solemn had he been at a funeral. When he rose to make his remarks, he said he was glad to observe that in some respects we had improved; we did n't make as much noise with our boots as we had done, and we did n't lop on the desks as badly.

"But this," said he, holding up the girl solemnly, "this don't look quite right."

Will whispered, just so that I could hear, that he should like to know how it *ought* to look.

"If you waste your time and thoughts upon

such frivolities as this, what do you suppose you will be good for when you become men and women?"

"School committees," whispered Will. "Please, sir," said he, raising his hand, "that was n't made in school time."

"No, I hardly supposed as much; but the very fact of its having been brought into the school-room shows that your minds are not where they should be, — upon your studies. It shows," said he, looking squarely at Will, "that you don't appreciate the worth of your educational advantages."

"Please, sir," said Will, raising his hand again, "sh-sh-she is n't mine, anyway. She belongs to Cynthia Strong."

Some of the large boys and girls tittered. Cynthia looked savage.

Mr. Pomeroy laid down the girl, at that, and went to scolding us about our advantages. One of the girl's feathers had come off on his hands, and when he ran his fingers through his hair after ideas, the feather stuck on his forehead. There it kept bobbing up and down, and waving so kind of funny-like while he talked, that I snickered out. I pretended I'd sneezed, though, and used my handkerchief. When he finished talking, he invited Webster to rise and remark.

Webster rose, threw back his shoulders, and took a good look at us. Then he began. Gustus Hillman is practising short-hand, and took down parts of the speech. I copy it from his note-book.

"My friends, — nay, my more than friends, for you are to me like a band of brothers and sisters, — your faces are dear to me; your names are like household words upon my lips. I have gone out and come in with you here, in the years that are passed; I have sat as you now sit in these seats; studied the same lessons that you now study; played the same games that you now play on yonder common — "

"Not by a long John!" whispered Will.

"— and my deepest interests, my tenderest affections cling around you as — as — as clings the ivy around the oak. I shall never forget you, — *never!* So long as the mighty orbs in yonder firmament give light to man, — so long as Time, in his unending flight, wheels through the vast cycles of the future, — so long will a regard for you hold its seat within this manly bosom." Here Webster clapped his hand to his breast, and mussed the manly shirt-bosom. "I can understand all your feelings as you meet here from day to day. I know all your hopes and fears, your joys and sorrows, your aspirations and your disappointments; for I, too, have been a boy. Yes, thank God, I, too, have been a boy! and I have no words in which to express to you the overwhelming emotion which the remembrance of that fact has forced upon me to-day.

"I would especially admonish you not to be discouraged. What though the Temple of Wisdom lifts its glittering fane on summits that now seem to you inaccessible? We have all been obliged to toil up the rugged steeps of that acclivity. Plato and Socrates were once young like you. Cicero and Demosthenes acquired the elements of learning in their youth. Press forward, then, and you shall rise higher and higher, until your names shall shine as stars in the diadem of Fame. But, as the ancient Romans were in the habit of remarking, *tempus fugit*, and I will not trespass further. Accept my heartfelt wishes for your prosperity and success in whatever pursuit in life you may in future engage."

Daniel Webster sat down, and stillness reigned. Will kept nudging me. The master closed the school. Webster came down from the platform and shook hands very kindly with all the large scholars. Most of the girls stood up stiff and awe-struck-like before him, as if he was the man who made the dictionary.

"Is n't Web a stunner, though!" said Will, after Webster and some of the large girls had started off.

"And what do you know about 'stunners,' pray?" asked Ed, putting his hand on Will's head and rumpling his hair over his eyes.

"I mean to be one myself one of these days. I shall come in to visit this school then, and if I don't spread and soar, then you never! and if I see a boy down on this row of seats who don't keep his nose clean nor anything I shall tell him I didn't enjoy any such advantages when I was of his age, and that he ought to improve 'em and fit himself for honor, glory, and immortality hereafter.

"And I tell you what 't is, Tommy Taylor, you won't be gone by that time, and if you don't nowadays mind your p's and q's a little better, I shall then just point this stern forefinger of mine at you and say, 'There 's a boy, who, if I mistake not, is in the broad road to destruction,' and I'll rake up all the old codgers on the face of the earth to hold up before you as examples, — Cicero, Demosthenes, and all the rest of 'em. I wonder who the deuce Cicero and Demosthenes *are*, anyway! I've heard about them ever since I was out of bibs."

"Ask Sue," said Homer; "she 's acquainted with all the self-educated men."

"Susanna Anastasia, who are Cicero and Demosthenes?" asked Will.

Sue was just going out. She turned round towards us, sniffed up her sharp nose, and says she, "Heathen!"

"Does she mean they or us, I wonder?" said Will, looking puzzled.

"There, now," continued he, swinging his book and slate over his shoulder, "I'm going through complex fractions to-night like a pig through a briar-lot. Come on, boys!"

We all filed out-of-doors. I ran back to get my handkerchief, and Tommy Taylor was up before the master's desk, kind of humble and cast-down like.

"Please, sir," said he, "if you'll give me my 'lasses-candy girl, I'll never bring her to school long as I live and breathe."

Tommy lives on the same street that I do, and that night I saw him out back of his father's barn, eating down the girl,—feathers, charcoal, lint, and all.

CHAPTER V.

FOREBODINGS AND FESTIVITIES.

TUESDAY morning Mike Flaherty came around with invitations to Charley Payson's birthday party. It was to be on Friday. My mother said she wanted me to go, but she did n't know what I had to wear. "Your best clothes looked so shabby I was ashamed of them last Sabbath," said she. "His father is going to get him a suit in Boston, next week, you know, Lovisa."

Aunt Lovisa did n't say whether she knew or not. She was crocheting a tidy, and when she 's at work on tidies she don't seem to think anything else is of any consequence.

Mother went up-stairs and brought down the clothes. She looked them over herself, and then held them up for Aunt Lovisa to look at.

Aunt Lovisa just glanced at them.

"The sleeve edges are badly worn, but I suppose we might bind them," said mother.

"Yes, we might," said Aunt Lovisa, spreading the tidy out in her lap.

"But here's this three-cornered rent in the jacket, and the pantaloon knees are just about worn through. They look rusty, upon the whole, don't they?"

"Yes, they do," said Aunt Lovisa, comparing a skein of worsted with that in her tidy.

"Mrs. Payson is so nice about Charlie's dress, too, and all that Boston company there," continued mother.

"I shan't have to stay at home, shall I, mother? These clothes look well enough, I'm sure," said I, holding the clothes up to me, and standing off at the farther side of the room.

"No, they don't; they're in no way suitable to wear to a party," said my mother.

I went to school feeling pretty down-hearted. All the boys were talking about the party and I could n't say anything; but when I went home to dinner father said he would go to Boston Wednesday and come back Thursday evening, so that I could have my clothes for Friday.

After that no one talked more about the party than I did.

All our class were invited. Mrs. Payson had requested the master to excuse us from afternoon session, and we were going as early as three o'clock. Mike told Will, who is always a kind of committee of inquiry upon such occasions, that the table was to be set under the trees; that Mr. Payson had bought a box of oranges and a dozen pineapples, and that the ice-cream and cake were to be sent up from the city.

My father did n't come Thursday evening, and I went to school Friday morning feeling blue again. I had on my best suit, and I finally asked Charlie if he did n't think those clothes would do.

"I know they don't look nice, but when I get on my ruffled shirt and best boots they 'll look some better," said I, brushing off the dust.

"Do? Of course they will," replied Charlie. "Who cares anything about clothes, anyway?"

Still I felt badly, and when I went home at noon and mother said father had n't come, I came near crying.

"Maybe he 's come, and stopped at the bank," said I.

She said it might be, but she was afraid not; I might run down and see. Will went with me. Father was n't there, and the teller said he had n't been there.

"What *shall* I do, Willie?" asked I.

"Go! If you have to wear your grandfather's double gown, *do you go*."

As soon as I got back to the house I asked mother if I could go and wear those clothes.

"Charlie thought they looked well enough, and Will said he would go if he was in my place," pleaded I.

She seemed to think it would n't do.

"Could n't you sponge 'em, mother?"

She smiled, and shook her head. Finally she said I might ask Aunt Lovisa what she thought about them. Aunt Lovisa looked me over, and turned me around, and looked me over again.

"I should n't want to go if I were you, Rob," said she at last. "It 's too warm a day. Stay at home and be a good boy; you can have some fruit and nuts, set the table in the yard, invite Katie Patterson and Freddy, and have a party by yourself."

Katie Patterson is five years old and brother Freddy four!

As soon as we were through dinner I ran to the depot and waited for the two-o'clock train. A number of people got off, but my father was n't among them. I started back. A company of boys and girls who had come from Graceville to attend the party were just ahead of me. They were nicely dressed, and I saw that my clothes would look too rusty. I could n't hold in any longer, and I cried all the way home.

"He has n't come, mother, and I can't go!" said I, choking, as I went into the sitting-room.

There he stood. He had jumped off the rear car as soon as the train slackened, and had cut across to the house the nearest way.

"I'm afraid it was an extravagant purchase," said my mother, as she unfolded the suit.

"No, I think not," said my father. "It must serve to remind Rob that he is n't to be called up in school again."

I threw my arms around his neck and kissed him over and over again. "I'll never be called up again as long as I live, — not if I can help it, father."

"That'll do," said he.

My suit fitted perfectly, and after cooling off and dressing I started for Mr. Payson's.

Charlie and Will came down the walk to meet me. Will put his finger on my buttons, and asked whether I was the Emperor of Russia or the Sultan of Turkey.

The party, consisting of about twenty-five boys and girls, was under the trees in the yard east of the house. Provisions were made there for all sorts of games, and we played many of our own introduction.

When we were redeeming forfeits, Nellie Royce and I were sent down to the brook to make a "double and twisted bow-knot." A "double and twisted bow-knot" is made by taking hold of hands and ducking your heads under your arms and through your arms, and kissing each other every time you go up or come down.

"I don't think it was nice to send us off so, do you, Rob?" asked Nellie, as soon as we were out of hearing of the party.

"I don't know as there's anything so bad about that. I'd much rather do what we're to do than to recite poetry for a forfeit," said I, throwing a pebble at a chipmunk on the wall.

"Now, Rob," said she, when we reached the brook, "let's just give each other one kiss, and have no arm-twisting about it."

She put out her red lips and I paid my forfeit, and a robin on a willow near sang, Tra-la-la-la!

"Is n't the brook pretty?" said she. "Let's just run up to that pool under the willow and see if there are any fish there."

When we returned the party were all sitting on the grass playing "Consequences." Will said we had been gone long enough to tie a whole clothes-line into double bow-knots. Just then Rose Payson stole up behind him and gave a most unearthly squawk on a blade of grass.

Will chased her into the flower-garden, where she dodged behind the bee-hives. Bees are always angry at Will, and he dare n't follow; so she sat among the flowers in her blue silk flounces, her lace handkerchief thrown over her head, and squawked at him to her heart's content. By the time they came back we were all playing on grasses, and it was proposed that Will and Rose should choose sides and play a match.

Rose showed us where we could find some particularly fine blades, and after we had gathered a supply we ranged ourselves in two rows over against each other, and Rose sounded the prelude. Will followed; then Rose and her side opened up; then our side; then Rose's; and the squeaking, the squawking, and squalling was awful. The people came out of the house, and one gentleman offered a lovely little pearl-handled knife to the winning side.

Then the way our grasses screeched, screamed, whistled, and wailed was quite appalling. Some of us were on a high pitch and some on a low, some made hoarse sounds, some sharp, and some shrill; we all played with all our might. Mr. Payson laughed until he cried.

The prize was given to Will. He attempted to present it to Rose, going down on one knee with a great flourish; but he struck upon a bumble-bee, and came up less gracefully than he went down, but Rose secured the knife.

After that we broke up in groups and sat around under the trees. Charlie invited us into the garden and showed off his own private little patch. He was very generous in giving us tastes of things, and if a boy praised up anything he offered him some seed!

We went to the carriage-house to see his new wheelbarrow. He had that morning painted it a bright blue, streaked off with yellow, and on each side the name, Rose, in yellow letters.

"I was going to name it after sister Mabel, but she said she must decline that honor, so I've called it Rose," said Charlie.

Will and Tommy Taylor got blue paint on their jacket-sleeves, and had to retire to the house and be rubbed up with benzine.

While the table was being set in the yard, we had music and dancing and a fine time in the parlor. When supper was announced Will had his wits about him and asked to take out Rose, but I made no move until Mrs. Royce touched me on the shoulder, and said she, "Won't you give your arm to the little girl in the striped dress, Robbie?"

The girl in the striped dress was Cynthia Strong.

Will gave my jacket a sly twitch as I crossed over to her. She did n't say a word to me, but thrust her arm up to the elbow through mine. She is taller and every way larger than I, and I can't think we looked very well together. She hardly spoke all the time we were at the table, but sat with her head thrown back and her nose turned up in the air. She seemed to feel that some one was imposing upon her. I'm sure it was n't I.

The table looked beautifully and we had a fine time at it. When we were nearly through, a Boston boy, Charlie's cousin, rose with his glass of lemonade and proposed Charlie's health.

We had all of us seen enough of the way grown people manage things to know that we ought to drink to the toast, but some did n't think quick enough, and it was three or four minutes before the last straggler set down his glass. Tommy Taylor, who always says the wrong thing in the wrong place, spoke up loud, and said he'd already drank so much lemonade it seemed as if he should burst.

We all pretended not to have heard Tommy's remark, and Charlie rose to respond to the sentiment.

I reckon his mother had taught him his speech beforehand.

As soon as Charlie sat down, Will hopped up with his glass, and says he, "To the prosperity of Charlie's whalebarrow. May it lead a long life and a useful one, do a good stroke of business and an honest one!"

The people under the trees applauded, and Tommy Taylor was just ready to cry "Hurrah!" but he sat beside me, and I slapped my hand over his mouth in time to prevent.

Some one called "Bob Brown, you speak to that! Bob Brown! Bob Brown!"

I can't think now how I dared, but then I

did n't feel afraid. I said the wheelbarrow was young yet, and we could n't be sure of its future, but we had great hopes for it. It had a good name, and if it did justice to its name, it would never disappoint our hopes.

We ate nuts for a while, and then a Graceville boy, who had been in a brown study, rose, glass in hand, and pompously proposed: "The fair sex: What should we men do without them?"

Quite a stir was made among the people under the trees. Mr. Payson called out that some one must respond to that, and Charlie invited Homer to speak.

Homer rose and hitched up his pantaloons — that 's a dreadful habit of Homer's. If he 's a little flurried, he begins to hitch up his pantaloons. He said he liked the fair sex very well, some of 'em much better than others, and he belived that was the way with everybody. He thought that as a general thing they were very useful about dusting, making pincushions, and lamp-mats, but come to cutting up stove wood or weeding in the garden, they were n't of much account. He had known a fair sex who could give a good ball; but come to marbles and nine-pins, they did n't amount to much again.

By the time the confectionery was passed we all felt some as Tommy did when we began drinking toasts. Charlie seemed to understand it, and invited us to fill our pockets to take home. We began stuffing away our candy, and a number put their cherries and an orange into their pockets.

The Boston boy began to look as if he had fallen among a lot of barbarians.

Some one mentioned that we had n't seen Charlie's presents, and we all jumped up from the table helter-skelter, and ran into the house. There was a rosewood writing-desk, a pencil-case, a cabinet-size portrait of Mrs. Payson, two or three books, a key-saw, a pair of sleeve buttons, two jackknives and a penknife.

Charlie said he thought the most of the key-saw, — Mike gave him that, — and Rose corrected him for expressing a preference.

We returned to the parlor, and Mabel gave us some music. Rose, Nellie, and Mollie Hammond each played a little. The train on which the Graceville boys and girls had to leave was due soon after sundown, and Mrs. Payson sent them to the depot in the carriage. The rest of us stayed until twilight.

When Aunt Lovisa saw how much candy I had brought home, she said she should be forever and ever ashamed of me; but she ate what I had in one pocket, and I gave mother and Freddy the remainder.

CHAPTER VI.

WILL AND I TAKE A RIDE.

I DIDN'T see Will again until three o'clock the next day. Then I found him under one of the horse-sheds back of his father's store. Capt. Parker's old mare and the wagon with the colt-skin robe stood under the shed.

"The captain has sued uncle 'Zekiel Wood, and the lawyers are holding a court in the Town Hall. This team has been here ever since morning," said Will, as I went in.

He was punching the mare in the sides and feeling her bones. He said he wished the master would engage her for the school to study anatomy upon. "She has thirty-five ribs," said he, counting up and down her back, "and lots of knobs and hollow places."

He went around to her head and opened her mouth. "My eyes! Do but see her teeth. She must be a revolutionary pensioner."

I went around and looked at her teeth, and then he wanted me to put my hand under her chops and see what a curious place there was there.

He poked, punched, and thumped her over, tickled her nose with straws, and fed her oats out of his hand. Then he proposed that we should back her out and take a ride around Barebones Hill.

"Oh, I should n't dare," said I.

"What are you afraid of? Here she 's occupied my father's shed and cribbed this feed-box all day. It 's no more than right that I should have a ride out of her."

"But the captain!" gasped I.

"He need n't know it. We 'll take our little airing and be back long before the lawyers are through with him and 'Zekiel."

While talking he had taken the mare by the bits and backed her out.

"Don't, Will, *don't!*" pleaded I.

"Don't get excited or be goosey-poosey, Bobby. Come on! She 's a regular staver for travel, and steady as a cow. We 'll rattle around and be back here in twenty minutes. Let me tumble you in. There you go!" Will pushed me in and jumped in after me.

He gathered up the reins and chirruped to the mare. She slowly straightened her limbs, stretched herself, and jogged out into the street.

"She don't start off as she does with the captain," said I.

"When we get a little out of the village I'll just touch her up with the whip," said Will.

"At this rate we never shall get out of the village; and oh, Will, everybody is looking at us. Do make her go faster."

Will twitched the reins and chirruped; she did n't mind it in the least. He took out the whip and struck her on the flank; she did n't pay any attention to it. We dragged by the bank. My father was standing in the door.

"Where are you going, Bob?" called he.

"Up to Capt. Parker's," said I.

Now, Capt. Parker's lay off in a different direction entirely, but the question had come so suddenly that I did n't know what to say.

"Oh, dear, Will!" exclaimed I, "I 've told father a lie."

Will made no reply, but rose on his feet and gave the mare a crack over the head. She started up so suddenly that he was thrown back on the seat, and my head was nearly jerked off. For a few minutes she travelled as I have seen her with the captain; but it had been much better fun to watch the captain jolt along than it was to be in the wagon ourselves. The old thing did n't seem to have any springs, and we had to hold on to the sides to keep from being bounced out. Every now and then Will would ask me if I did n't enjoy it. I said I did.

"Why don't you talk more, then?" asked he.

I said I did n't feel like talking.

We struck off on to the Barebones Hill road. "Now for some fun!" said Will, trying to be gay.

I wanted to ask him to let me get out and go back to my father, but was ashamed to do it.

The road was sandy and had but few houses and no shade-trees.

"No one around here to see us," said Will.

"No," said I.

"Are n't you having a good time, Bob?" asked he, looking around into my face.

"Yes."

"What makes you sigh so much, then?"

"Oh!" said I, "she goes so slow!"

Will took out the whip and struck her across the back, across the flank, across the sides. We each of us tried punching her with the butt end of the whip. Sometimes she would start up and trot for a rod or two; then would drop her head, and fall into that dreadful jog. The sand was deep and burning hot; the sun blazed like a great fire; we were both covered with dust, my head ached, and Will's face was turning lobster-color.

"I 'm afraid we shall be sun-struck. Is n't there *any*thing that can be done to get this horse along faster?"

"Nothing, unless we get out and carry her," said Will. "I believe I 'll try another crack over her head. Hold on to your seat, Bob."

I grasped the back of the wagon. Will

partly rose, and holding on to the dash-board with one hand, with the other gave the mare a blow. She sprang, something cracked, something crashed; the forepart of the wagon sank down. The mare was angry and rushed ahead. Will pulled on the reins, I shouted "Whoa!" the cracking and crashing went on.

When she was ready the mare came to a stand-still, shook her head, and looked back at us as if she would like to know if we were satisfied *now!* We jumped out and made an examination. The axle of the wagon was broken, and there seemed to be a general splintering up of things, and many loose irons.

"What *are* we going to do?" gasped I.

Will thought I should have to stay with the horse while he ran back to the nearest house for help.

The nearest house was a quarter of a mile back, but in plain sight. I took the marc by the bits and watched Will as he ran off through the dust. He rang at the front door of the house, he knocked at the back door, but no one answered; he peeped in at a window, and then turned and made signs to me that there was no one at home, and he was going on to the next house. It was a half-mile between the two. It was hot, *hot* there in the road. The fiies bit the mare, and I every minute expected that she would start and run.

I felt pretty sure that we should have to pay for the wagon. I did n't know how much such a wagon was worth, but I knew our new phaeton cost more than two hundred dollars. Supposing the captain asked a hundred for this, or seventy-five or even fifty, would n't my father be obliged to pay it? — my dear father, who, only the day before, had bought me those nice clothes! Maybe, too, he would have to pay for the horse. I did n't know what kind of a claim the captain would set up; he had the reputation of being a hard man. Then suddenly it flashed across me that he might arrest us for stealing the team! Had the mare started at that moment I could n't have held her. Will and I should be thieves, then, and have to be tried before a court and sent to the state-prison! Oh, how my mother would feel! and it would break my father's heart; it would kill them all, Freddy and grandma — what would grandma say? I thought I should die! It might be that the court was already out, and the captain had missed his horse, and the constables were after us. Oh! how hot it was!

As far down the road as I could see rose up a cloud of dust. I knew there was a team in it. It was coming for me! On it came, nearer and nearer, and I shook like a leaf. I knew how it would be: the constable would jump out, grab me, perhaps put on the handcuffs, and tumble me into his buggy, heels over head, hit or miss. I wondered if he had already taken Will. I could see the horse, a black horse, — not like the constable's, like the deputy sheriff's though; no, the man was not as large as the sheriff. My heart gave a bound; he was a stranger!

"Hallo, Bub! you 've had quite a smash-up," said he. "Can I do anything to help you?"

"No, sir, I thank you. Another man has gone back after help," said I, shaking all over, and standing stock-still in the middle of the road.

"Well, can't you move your calabash a little, so that I can get by?"

I led the mare into the ditch, and the man passed on. A few minutes more, and another cloud of dust appeared. This proved to contain two ladies. They drove slowly, stared at me, and said something that sounded like "That 's the boy they 're hunting for."

At last came Will, and with him Mr. Noah Johnson's hired man, 'Bijah Whittlesey. 'Bijah is a slow, hulking, prying fellow. It seemed to me that he would be about the poorest help we could have, but I was glad to see any one.

"Jehosiphat!" said he, as he came up and surveyed the wreck, "if this is n't the capen's old go-cart! And all gone to thunder in this style! How came the capen to let you youngsters be trucking around with it?"

"Please, Mr. Whittlesey," said Will, in his smoothest way, "don't ask us any questions. Just help us out of the scrape, and we 'll reward you handsomely."

'Bijah pulled up his cap and scratched his head.

"This 'ere is pretty considerable of a smash-up, now le' me tell you; and if you boys have been raisin' the devil with the capen's property unbeknownst to him, I don't know wh'er or not I ought to help ye."

"O Mr. Whittlesey," said I, "we did n't mean any harm; we only thought we 'd take a ride. Do *please* help us."

"The capen sets a heap by that old critter and the wagin. He 's druv' 'em going on now five-and-twenty years. The capen 's a master hand for lawin' it, too, and I don't know as I want to be mixed up in any of his musses. Ye see I 'm of age, and he might hold me liable."

"Mr. Whittlesey, your name shall never be mentioned in connection with this affair. I give you my word of honor as a gentleman that it shall not," said Will.

"Wa-al, seein' it 's little Bob here who 's in the scrape, I dunno but I must try to give you a lift. He 's the boy who helped pick up my potatoes when they spilled out of the bags going down Town-Hall hill last winter."

"Yes; I am that boy, I am. Mr. Whittlesey, do please help us, — quick, please, won't you?"

"Must n't be in too big a hurry. I shall have to go back for a rope and some spikes. I thought by what Bill, here, said it could n't be much of a smasher, an' I did n't bring anything but a hammer and a few shingle-nails."

I was every minute expecting the constable along.

"Can't you possibly repair the wagon without going back?" asked I.

"Lordy massy, no; an' I dunno as I can then, but I'll try. The wagon 's been a shiftless, rickety old thing these ten years. Nobody but the capen could a-kept it together. I'll start along in a minute, soon 's I get cooled off a little; I swaow, though, there ain't much chance for coolin' here. Old mare looks as if she was about done for. You 'd better take her out of the thills and tie her under that apple-tree over in the pasture."

I went off into the pasture with the mare, and when I returned 'Bijah had gone.

"At the rate he was walking when he went

out of sight, it'll take him an hour to get around," said Will gloomily.

"Let's run away," said I.

"Where can we run to?"

"Anywhere, — to Boston or to sea."

"We should be sorry, and come back again if we started."

"We shall be sorry if we hang around here until we're arrested."

"Arrested! They can't arrest us for an accident," said Will.

"They can call it stealing a horse and buggy, and arrest us for that," said I.

That idea startled Will a little. He picked up a stalk of grass and began chewing it vigorously.

"I don't believe it," said he. "They shan't arrest you, anyway, Bob; I'll swear to the very last that you didn't want to come. I won't let them take you. And they shan't have me, either," added he, kicking at the wagon. "I'm more afraid father will have to pay for the *blarsted* old thing. I wish the lightning would strike it!"

"Oh, don't, Will! What would become of us?"

"Well, let's do what we can towards patching it up with the nails 'Bije left," said he.

"Then you think we'd better stay by, do you?"

"Stay by? Yes. I'll see the thing out if they hang me for it."

Our hammering only seemed to make matters worse with the wagon, and we finally sat down and waited for 'Bijah.

"Cooler 'n 't was at noon," said he, pushing his hat back and wiping off the perspiration as he came up.

"Yes," said we. "How long do you think it'll take you to mend the wagon?"

"Wa'al, I dunno; dunno 's I can fix it at all, still, maybe I can kinder cobble it up so 't you can get home. Feel a leetle scared, don't ye now? Dunno 's I wonder. Capen don't let up easy when he gets a grip on a feller."

"You don't think he'll shut us up, do you, Mr. Whittlesey?" asked I.

"I guess not, still I can't tell. Boys must

learn not to meddle with things that don't belong to 'em."

We said we never should again.

In about half an hour 'Bijah had rigged up the wagon so that he said we might try it.

"It's a mighty ticklish consarn to draw a mile and a half, now I tell you; but if you drive slow, and are careful in going over the thankee-marms, and don't run on to no stones, I guess you can get her thar," said he, as we started off.

I led the mare by the bits. Will walked by the side of the wagon, and kept watch of it. 'Bijah went with us a half-mile or more.

"'T ain't no use telling you to go slow, for you can't go no other way," said he, as he bade us good-by. "'T would n't take much to send the old thing to pieces again; but houses 'll be gettin' thicker an' thicker, so 't if wuss comes to wuss you can get some one to put you together again."

We thanked 'Bijah again, and Will offered to pay him; but he said no, he should n't "tax nothing."

We drove very slowly, and it was nearly sundown when we entered the village. I felt as if I should sink with mortification. We neither of us looked either to the right hand or to the left. As we passed Dr. Hammond's, Ed and Gustus Hillman, who were standing in the door, called out to us, but we pretended not to hear them. As we went by the bank I saw my father sitting by the window. It was past bank hours; he must have been there watching for us. As we came in sight of the store I saw the piazza was filled with men.

"There they are, Will," said I.

"Who are?"

"Why, the authorities."

"I can't help it if they are. Don't you be frightened, Bob; you were n't to blame."

The men were looking at us. It seemed as if the old mare would never, never get there. I had half a mind, even then, to turn and run. As we came nearer I saw the men were laughing.

"You've had a pretty sorry time, have n't you, Bob?" said Lawyer Royce, taking his cigar from his mouth as I led up the horse.

"Yes, sir," said I, looking down at the piazza steps.

"We've brought your horse back for you, Capt. Parker," said Will, as if it was all a good joke that the captain must enjoy.

"Yes, you've brought the horse back and you've brought the wagon back, and the wagon is as 't is, you young rascal! You ought to be trounced, severely trounced!"

The captain collared Will as if he was going to "trounce" him then and there. At this Mr. Bradley stepped forward.

"Let alone the boy, captain; I'll attend to him. You make out your bill for damages."

At the mention of bill the captain let go of Will and began to examine the wagon.

"If any one'll go for my father he'll pay my part," said I, feeling as if I was in some way a prisoner and should n't myself be allowed to go for him.

"Bob is n't to blame, father; he ought not to pay anything. I made him go," said Will.

"I'll see your father if I think best," said Mr. Bradley, speaking to me, but not looking at either of us.

The captain said that he "guessed upon the hull five dollars would pay for damages to the wagon, but there was the old mar'. She's a mighty nervous beast and ain't used to boys. Boys ain't nowise careful with critters. Her nerves may be onsettled for life by this 'ere scrape. Three dollars for damages to the mar', 'squire."

Mr. Bradley counted out eight dollars and tendered it to the captain.

"Will that be satisfactory?"

"Wa'all, yes, so far as the team is consarned, that's satisfactory; but there's my time ought to be wuth something. I've been waiting now since four o'clock. Say a dollar for my time, 'squire."

All the men laughed. Mr. Bradley handed the captain the dollar.

"Better pass the establishment over to the boys now, Parker; you've got a fair price for it," said one man.

"I've a calabash that I'd like to dispose of at the same rate. Call on me when you want another ride, boys," said another.

Mr. Bradley pointed his finger at Will, and said he, "You, sir, start for home!"

We both started.

"We are coming out better than I expected," said I, as soon as we were out of hearing.

"Don't you s'pose I 'll catch it?" replied he.

"Of course; but that is n't so bad as going to prison."

"No; 't is n't as bad," said Will, gloomily.

CHAPTER VII.

CONSEQUENCES OF OUR RIDE.

WHEN I reached home I found father had come before me, and I walked directly into the room where he was. I wanted he should "settle" with me as soon as possible. I stood for half a minute, cap in hand, before him. He just looked up, and said he, "You 're late, Bob, and you look rather begrimed. You 'd better go and wash, and then ask mother for your supper."

I washed and brushed up, and went into the dining-room. Mother did n't say much to me. She looked as if she had been crying.

As soon as I had eaten what little I wanted, I went back into the sitting-room; but no one paid any attention to me. Father was playing with Freddy just as he used to play with me. I went up and stood beside them, but they did n't say anything to me. I stole away and sat down in a corner. The lamps were lighted and the room looked bright and cheerful, but I sat back among the shadows, winking and winking, swallowing and swallowing. Finally I felt so miserable I walked up to my father, and said I, "Will and I drove around Barebones Hill with Capt. Parker's mare this afternoon."

"Indeed!" said he, without looking up. "Sister Lovisa, won't you read aloud what the *Republican* says about the doings at Charleston?"

Aunt Lovisa opened the paper with much rustling, folded it down, and began reading in an emphatic voice that struck terror to my soul.

I slunk back in the corner and sat with my arms folded and my feet on the chair-round until nine o'clock. Then I slipped out without bidding any one good-night, and went to bed in the dark. I dreamed that Will and I were fastened to the old mare's heels, and she was dragging us around Barebones Hill, while the captain sifted red-hot ashes over us.

The next morning was pleasant, but I could n't enjoy it. Father treated me just as usual.

Mother looked sober, but let me have all the honey I wanted on my griddle-cakes. I did n't want as much as usual. Aunt Lovisa was in excellent spirits, and I felt sure justice was going to be executed upon me. How I did wish it might be over with!

I went to church, and when we were going down to Sabbath School, Will whispered and asked me if I'd "had my licking yet." "I had a regular dresser last night, and feel stiff as the old mare this morning. I never want to set eyes on either her or the captain again," said he.

I should have been willing to take two or three dressers if I could have had the thing off my mind.

Miss Lane asked me who slew Goliath, and I answered "Moses." Then all the boys giggled, and Tommy Taylor told her over again what I'd said, — as if she'd been deaf the first time.

After tea that night my father invited me into the parlor, and I knew my time had come. When the shutters are closed our parlor is a solemn place, and my father gave me a solemn talk.

He said that taking the captain's team was stealing the use of property, and that it was but a step from that to stealing the property itself. He said Will's having tempted me was no excuse; every one who did wrong was in some way tempted to it. He said he should n't punish me for going off with the team, because I had already been sufficiently punished. He was glad that it was so; he wanted me to learn that God had so arranged the laws of the universe that every wrong act brings its own punishment, just as putting one's fingers in the fire burns them. He said that if Will and I had had a nice ride, and no one had found out about it, we should still some time have suffered from the injury done our moral nature.

He said the lie I told him also brought its own penalty, but because I was n't likely to feel that at present, he must punish me in a way that I could understand and remember, and that would prevent my telling more lies and doing myself more injury.

He made me feel that a falsehood was a very serious affair. I did n't quite understand all he said; but when he told me that I was to be shut up all day Monday and have nothing to eat but bread and water, I understood perfectly. However, I felt quite happy when I knew my fate, and Freddy and I got up in a big chair, had a meeting, and sang, —

"There is a happy land,
Far, far away,
Where saints in glory stand,
Bright, bright as day."

At eight o'clock the next morning Aunt Lovisa came up to my room with my breakfast, which was two thick slices of bread and a glass of water. She said I was to eat it in the little back chamber, where my father said I was to spend the day. I took the waiter from her and walked into the little room with all the dignity I could command. She locked the door and went away.

I sat down on the bed, and having placed the waiter in the chair before me played that I was a prisoner shut up in a tower, and Aunt Lovisa was my keeper and had just brought me a mouldy crust and a jug of water.

After I had eaten I sat down by the window. It overlooked our back yard and Tommy Taylor's father's yard. I heard a great crowing and cackling among Mr. Taylor's fowls; finally, one cock flew upon the wall and came flopping down through the clothes-line into our yard. Then he stretched his neck and gawky legs and ran for our garden. He began scratching in a musk-melon hill. The musk-melons are Aunt Lovisa's. She 's very fond of them, and at first I felt sorry that he had gone at them; then I remembered how grimly she had marched me into confinement, and I felt wicked, and said, "Go it, Cocky!"

He had uprooted one melon-hill and damaged another, when the back door opened, and Aunt Lovisa charged out upon him. I had great fun in watching her chase him about the garden: usually it is I who have to run after the fowls. She drove him home and had an interview with Mrs. Taylor. Mrs. Taylor caught and thrust him under the bushel-basket, and I saw no more of him.

By and by I lay down on the bed and went

to sleep. Aunt Lovisa woke me by bringing in the bread and water for my dinner. A few minutes after she left, mother came up softly and brought me a saucerful of peas and a bit of beefsteak. She said she did n't think it was good for the health to go all day without something warm and nourishing.

I threw my arms around her neck and hugged and kissed her. She said that if I thought I could remember and never tell a lie again she would ask my father to let me come down to tea. I said I thought I could remember.

In the afternoon my room grew dull. I could n't see any one from the window, though I put my head out as far as I dared. I could n't find anything in the bureau drawers but bed-linen. I lay down on the bed and counted the specks and spots on the ceiling. I turned over and studied the carpet. I went to the window and stretched my head out again, but could hear nothing, see nothing. I wished the rooster could get out. I could n't go to sleep; I could n't scare up a fly. It seemed to me that if I was n't let out at tea-time I should die.

I was thrumming on the window-sill and counting off time when a chip whizzed just past my ear and struck against the window-frame. I looked down in the yard, and saw Will with a basket of eggs on his arm.

"In solitary confinement, are you, Bob?"

I replied that I was.

"I suspected as much. I've had an eye out for you ever since school closed. I had these eggs to take over to Mr. Hammond's, and I thought I'd just take the back of your house on my way. Having a serious time of it, are n't you?"

"Oh! it's dreadful, Will. I'd rather take a dozen whippings."

"Not if you had my father to lay 'em on, I reckon. When I come back from Dr. Hammond's can't I in some way get up there and 'liven you up a little?"

"No, no! Don't try it; I would n't have you for anything," said I; "I've made up my mind never to do anything bad again."

"Well, I've made up my mind never to tempt you, and I hope nobody'll tempt me, for this is going to be just about as much of a load as I can carry. I 've got to pay my father the captain's charges, and I 've turned in all my molasses money, my half-dollar with the hole in it, and all my coppers, and there 's four dollars and eighty-seven cents due yet. I 've got to work that out of my legs, running errands and the like."

"I shall turn in what money I have, but it is n't much. Aunt Lovisa made me put twenty-five cents into the contribution box last Sunday," said I.

"You won't do any such thing, Bobby; I shan't let you. This is my debt of honor, and it would n't be proper for you to meddle with it. My self-respect won't allow it. What have you had to do up there all day?"

"Nothing."

"What have you had to look at?"

"There was Mrs. Taylor's rooster, but she shut him up under the bushel-basket."

"Under that?" asked Will, nodding towards the basket.

"Yes."

"I'll tip it over and let him out if you say so."

"No, no," said I, "don't let's get into any more scrapes."

"That's so. You're going to be my guardian angel, aren't you, Bobby? No more scrapes for me till I get my debts paid."

Just then we heard a door open and shut below stairs. Will thought some one was coming out the back way, and started to run. He tripped, and fell on his face. Some of the eggs broke in the basket and some rolled out and broke.

"Jerusalem!" gasped he, struggling up and wiping the yolk off his face with his jacket-sleeve. "There goes fifty cents more!"

Just then mother came out. "O Will, poor boy!" said she.

She picked up the eggs that were on the ground, took the basket, and went into the house with him. Pretty soon he came out looking clean and fresh and with his basket filled up again.

"Look there!" said he. "She took out all

the cracked and broken ones, washed off the others, and gave me enough to make up my two dozen. She's one of the salt of the earth!"

Off he went, whistling, dancing on one foot, and swinging his basket in a way that threatened to upset the two dozen again.

Not very long after, mother called me to tea. We had it earlier and it was a rather nicer tea than usual. Mother let me eat two tarts at the table, and after tea, when there was no one in the room but she and I, she said I might have another if I wished.

Father played backgammon with me in the evening, and we had very nice times.

CHAPTER VIII.

I AM CARED FOR.

MOTHER poached the eggs she had taken out of Will's basket for breakfast the next morning, and gave me all I wished. Afterwards I had the headache, and Aunt Lovisa said it was for no other reason than because I had eaten too much egg, and she did n't see how parents could go on pampering the appetites of their children when they every day saw the ill effects of it.

By nine o'clock my head ached so badly that mother said I need n't go to school. It did n't feel much better by afternoon, but mother and Aunt Lovisa had an invitation out to tea, and did n't consider me sick enough to prevent their going. Freddy was to stay with me, and mother said she would stop at Mr. Bradley's and ask to have Will come over after school.

"I have laid supper for Will on the little

table," said she, "and if you wish for anything to eat, Robbie, you must ask him to toast you a slice of bread."

Aunt Lovisa came along just then, and lifted the napkins mother had spread over Will's supper. "Quince preserves and *three kinds of cake!*" said she to herself.

After they had put on their bonnets and shawls mother kissed me, Aunt Lovisa charged me against eating any preserves if I did n't want a worse headache than I had, and they both started. At five o'clock Will came running and puffing up the street, hands in his pockets as usual.

"I had to carry a bundle of dry goods up to Mrs. Davis, and could n't come as early as I wished," said he. "Now, where 's that bread?"

"What bread?"

"Your mother left word that I was to toast you a slice of bread, and I want to do it, and have it off my mind."

I said I did n't wish for toast; should n't eat it if I had it.

"Can't help that. I make it a point nowadays to obey orders and ask no questions."

He cut a slice of bread about three quarters of an inch thick, and whisked off into the kitchen. Fred and I followed.

Will threw open the stove-doors, ran a silver fork through the bread, and set it toasting. It burned, but he scraped off the black; it fell off the fork and broke, but he picked out the pieces and blew off the ashes. He turned cold water on it, and set it in the oven to warm while he made the tea.

"They said 'Put in a teaspoonful of tea,' but they did n't tell how much water. I should think a dipperful would be enough, should n't you?"

I said I should, and he poured in the dipperful, and sat down on the floor to wait for it to boil. Every now and then he twitched up the cover to report progress. As soon as the teapot began to sing he snatched it off, and poured me out a cup of tea. It was very light-colored, and Will said he was afraid it was n't very strong, but he would put in two teaspoonfuls of sugar, and make it good.

After he had prepared the tea he brought me my toast. The plate was very hot on one side, but the toast was n't hot anywhere. The butter stuck around in little lumps that would n't melt. It tasted a little smoky and a little of ashes. I tried to eat it, to please Will, but could n't, and I gave it to Freddy, who had been looking on as if he thought it must be a great treat. He and Will spread preserves all over it and ate it between them. They also drank my tea.

The fire made my headache worse and worse, and Will grew alarmed about me. He said I ought to go to bed and have a jug of hot water at my feet; his grandmother, when she was sick, always had a jug of hot water at her feet.

"O Will!" said I, "I won't."

"S'posin' you should have a shock? Then I guess you 'd wish you 'd done something. You see, you 're sick, Bob, and if you don't keep your feet warm, it 's liable to go to your head."

Then he told me of ever so many old ladies who had had shocks sitting in their chairs, and who, he was pretty sure, would n't have had them had they been in bed with jugs of hot water at their feet.

He talked so much about it and seemed so

confident that it was the right thing and the only right thing to do, that I finally consented to be put to bed in mother's room. Will was exceedingly energetic in getting me in, and he spread an extra blanket and two comfortables on the bed, and tucked me up until I thought I should melt. He said I must be kept warm, or it would "strike in." Then he bustled around after a jug. Fred was greatly excited about having a "chug," and helped him search. They found one up garret, but the water streamed out of that as fast as they turned it in. They finally took the vinegar jug.

"Don't that feel comfortable, sonny?" asked Will, after he had put it to my feet.

I tried to think it did, but as the jug was large and the water in it not warm, it really was not comfortable.

Will brought in a piece of plum-cake and his saucerful of preserves, and sat down at the head of my bed. Every once in a while he would ask me if I did n't feel better.

"You don't really think I shall have a shock, do you, Will?" asked I.

"No, I don't think you will, now. You can move both sides, can't you?"

I tried, and said I could.

Will said I must lie very quiet, and he undertook to tell me a story, but he had to stop so often to take a bite of cake or a spoonful of preserves that I did n't much enjoy the story.

"Feel any better, now?" asked he, as he scraped the last drop of juice from his saucer.

"No," said I, "I don't, Will; I feel sick, and my back aches."

"Back-ache? Dear me! That's a bad symptom."

He sat in a study for a minute or two, and then declared I must have a mustard paste on that back.

"No, *no*, Will," said I, "I don't want anything of the kind."

"S'posing you don't, Bob; it's what ought to be done, and it ought to be done *now*, before it's too late."

Off he started, with Fred at his heels, and I heard them rummaging the house after old cloth.

"Never mind, Freddy," said Will at last, "I 'll take my handkerchief."

Pretty soon he came in, with the handkerchief spread out in his two hands, the mustard running down his wrists and dripping on the carpet.

"It 's too thin," said he, "but we could n't find the mustard-box, and I emptied in here what was in the castor-bottle. It 's just the same thing, you know."

For all I could say to the contrary, he would apply it; and it was cold and ran down my side, and was n't nice at all. He felt sure, though, that it would help me; and after he had tucked me up again, smoothed my pillows, and sprinkled a little camphor over me, he seated himself and began telling me stories. Every time Fred stirred, he would stop and scold him and order him to keep still, so that I could go to sleep.

I did finally drop asleep, and when I awoke mother and Aunt Lovisa had returned. Mother was bending over me, with her hand on my forehead. Aunt Lovisa was lamenting over the state of the bedroom carpet.

I was quite sick through the night, and in the morning father sent for Dr. Hammond.

Will looked in on his way to school, and said my face was a regular magenta color. He offered to stay and help take care of me; but mother thanked him and declined.

Dr. Hammond said I had the scarlet fever. I was frightened at first, but the doctor said I was n't very sick and he 'd no thoughts of allowing me to be very sick; I was only going to be kept in the house and be waited upon, and have the parlor ornaments to look at; and he said I might order Aunt Lovisa around to my heart's content.

It seemed very strange that I did n't care more about looking at things that I want when I 'm well and can't have. It seemed strange, too, to have some one lying in the room with me all night, and to have the lamp burning, to feel hot and restless, and disturbed by noises, to be taking something out of a teaspoon every few minutes, and not wishing anything to eat.

Thursday, after school, Ed Hammond, Gustus Hillman, and Homer came in to see me.

Will could n't come because he 'd never had the fever.

Ed brought me some powders from his father, and he brought me a couple of illustrated papers and a letter from Will. Gustus gave me a pencil with a blue lead, and Home emptied his pockets on the table and offered me my choice of the articles. I did n't see anything I cared for but his pocket-rule, and I knew he prized that like the apple of his eye; so I said I would take his top. Then he marched up and gave me the rule also. It was very kind in him, and I invited him to come again; but mother said after he left that she could n't encourage his coming often, because he talked so loudly about "when he had the fever," and agitated me so badly. She liked Ed because he was quiet and gentle.

This is the note Will sent.

"THURSDAY AFTERNOON.

"DEAR BOB, —

"I 'm sorry you 're down, but I expected it. You did n't appear like yourself Tuesday, and I told Freddy while we were hunting for the jug,

'Freddy,' said I, 'he 's going to be sick.' Did you know I sent for your mother? After you went to sleep there, so like a little lamb, I took your wrist to feel your pulse, but I could n't find any pulse. That frightened me, for I knew what ailed old Mr. Newton when he died with the typhoid fever was, they could n't find any pulse; so I told Freddy to run as fast as he could and get your mother. Fred got lost, and there would have been bad times had n't Mr. Royce stumbled upon him, and known whose boy he was, and hunted up your mother. Do you have to take much medicine? Ed has some powders for you, and I tried to make him let me touch my tongue to them, just to see what you 've come to, but he would n't. If they 're bad, quince jelly is good to take the taste out.

"Do you know what brought it on? Father says it may be because I dragged you around Barebones Hill in the heat, and that it ought to be an awful warning to me. I hope 't was n't. I can't write any more now, for Ed is hurrying me up.

"Devotedly, affectionately, etc.,

"WILL."

Friday Ed called again and brought me his and Gustus's photograph albums to look at. He also brought me another letter from Will, — so long a one that mother had to read it to me.

"AT SCHOOL, FRIDAY AFTERNOON.

"First class in Grammar reciting, master scolding because they have n't looked out their parsing lessons, Almina Harris crying, Ike Tucker muttering.

"DEAR BOB, —

"Don't you wish you was here? I do. We 've got to stay after school to recite our Geography again. We 're in 'Sahara, or the Great Desert,' and it 's hard work getting through; we 're overwhelmed by clouds of sand, and are as badly off as the camel in the picture. I went down three in spelling to-day, and am now at the foot. Homer and I are going to have a dialogue next time we speak, David and Goliath. He 's David and I 'm Goliath. He 's the largest, but I 've the most voice and can deliver the challenge best.

"Did the thunder-shower Friday afternoon

shake your nerves any? Was n't it a stunner? We could n't see to study, and boys and girls had their recess together. The girls were some of them white, some green, and some blue. They huddled together, and kept saying, 'Oh! how dark!' 'What is coming?' 'Is there going to be a whirlwind?'

"Every time it thundered some of 'em would clap their hands over their ears. Rose and Nellie, with their arms around one another, sat on the top of a desk crying. Home and I tried to comfort 'em and raise their drooping spirits, but we were n't appreciated.

"Cynthia all at once started up and declared this pretending to be so afraid of thunder-showers, spiders, and snakes was all affectation; said she'd dare run down through the pine woods to Ferris's old grist-mill. Home stumped her to do it. Ike offered her a quarter if she would go down to the mill and back, and Sam Harris offered another quarter. The sky was black as ink, wind blowing, leaves and dust flying, lightning flashing, thunder crashing, and rain expected every minute; but Cynthia just threw on Almina Harris's old water-proof, and away she went. She came back a little after the first burst of rain, and brought a sprig of that elder that grows beside the mill. Is n't she a brick? We boys hurrahed for her.

"'How did it look among the pines?' asked Ike.

"'Dark,' said she. 'Where 's my money?'

"Before the rain was through, the school-house yard was full of little puddles, and the boys from Miss Rice's and Miss Mixer's schools came out under umbrellas and barefoot, and paddled around in the water. Tommy Taylor off with his shoes and stockings, rolled up his trowsers, and went in with them. I was just going in myself when the bell rang.

"The master thinks I've been long enough drawing my map of Sahara, and I shall have to read this to the school if I don't wind off.

"Y'rs devotedly,

"WILL.

"P. S. — Won't it be too bad if you lose the Fourth?"

For the next three days I was so sick that I lay in bed all day and had the room darkened. I did n't see or hear from any of the boys, though mother afterwards told me that they called at the back door to ask after me. Tuesday I was much better, and Ed came again, bringing me another letter, and a bouquet as large as a peck measure from Will.

"BOBBY DEAR, —

"I 've been greatly distressed because you 've been worse, but the doctor says this morning you 're coming out right, and my appetite is better. To-morrow is the Fourth. There is n't going to be much of a *sell*ebration. Fire-crackers are cheap, and if I was n't so badly in debt I should lay in heavily for them. Father says he will give me just one bunch and no more. That I call putting a fellow on a short allowance.

"I wish I had something to send you, but I have n't, so I send some flowers. I send you some of every variety I could get. That double sunflower is one I asked Mrs. Deacon Clapp for, especially for you; that green around it is southernwood; you 'll find some white rosebuds and a japonica Mrs. Royce sent; that red stuff between the *saffron* rose and the heliotrope is a bean blossom, — I got it off a vine that runs over the deacon's buttery window; you 'll find four different kinds of bachelor-buttons. I 've tied them up with my old hat-band. The hat is used up; it 's been breaking away and fraying out all along back. Yesterday I wet it through and through to keep my head cool, and when it got dry and stiff I sat down upon it by accident and smashed it all to flinders.

"Home has got three bunches of fire-crackers and a half dozen Catherine wheels. He is going to give you part. I don't suppose you can write, but send me some word by Ed.

'Y'rs affectionately,

"WILL."

Aunt Lovisa took the bouquet, and turned it around before her slowly. Then she looked up at Ed, and they both laughed. She was going to take the bouquet to pieces and assort the flowers, but I would n't allow her. I had it put in a big pitcher and set on my stand.

Mother was tired out and Aunt Lovisa had the headache, so Ed watched with me that night. He took excellent care of me. In the night, when I was restless, he rolled me up in a blanket, took me in his arms, and told me long, queer stories that put me to sleep.

CHAPTER IX.

CONVALESCING.

INDEPENDENCE day Homer stumbled into my room, knocking against the bedstead, tipping over a foot-stool, depositing his hat among my medicines, and finally presenting me with a lot of fireworks from himself and the other boys.

Will, Charlie, and Tommy Taylor, with mother's permission, came outside my window and looked in through the glass. Will said I looked the worse for wear. Charlie Payson said my chin had sharpened, but he could see that it was the same old fellow. Tommy wanted to know if my appetite had come yet. They all said they'd give considerable to have me out on the sidewalk again. They blew off their best fireworks for my edification, and with a series of elegant bows departed.

The latter part of the week I had more letters. Will wrote: —

"DEAR BOBBY, —

"I am staying in from recess in order to have a letter ready to send by Ed. Dr. Hammond says I exposed myself to the fever by going in to see you that first Wednesday morning. We 've got to miscellaneous examples in fractions, and I 'd as lief have a fever as not. We 're in periphrastic conjugations also, and the periphrastics are tremendous, Bob. We go in ten feet deep and don't strike bottom then. Conjugations and sour strawberries give me the colic so that I don't sleep nights; and if scarlet fever or something else don't set in I shan't stand it long.

"Won't the blanc-mange, canned peaches, and quince jelly that you 'll have when you begin to get better be nice?

"A fancy-goods dealer has moved into the corner store in Wheeler & Spooner's building, and he has some of the neatest hair-brushes you ever saw, — mirror in the back and comb in the side. I 've been in five times to ask the price of 'em. The last time he would n't show 'em to me; said he, 'If you want one of those brushes you can have it for a dollar and a half. If you don't want it, I don't want you running here twice a day to ask the price of 'em.'

"I told him I did want one, but I could n't command the necessary. That I thought would melt his heart, but it did n't. I can't have anything anyway. All the money I get has to go for damages to the old mare. I've sold my jackknife to Gustus for fifty cents and turned that towards the debt. They've got a lot of finger-rings at the new store, good as gold, and only a shilling apiece. Charlie has given one with a red stone in it to Nellie Royce. So what do you think of that, my boy? Fourth of July did n't amount to much, so you did n't lose anything there. School closes in two weeks.

"Yours, "WILLIAM."

I had a very nice letter from Charlie. Here is a part of it: —

. . . "Down in that glen back of our house I've found two black birch trees. The boys went down with me last night and got some bark. It's splendid, and I broke off two sticks to send you, but mother said you couldn't eat it. She is going to send you a lot of nice things by Mike.

"I have got a job with my wheelbarrow,—wheeling loam to put around the trees on the common. I worked every minute that I could get out of school yesterday, and earned forty-five cents. Mr. Spooner came across the common and said that when I was through with that job he should like to employ me to wheel groceries home to his customers. Mother and Mabel are mortified, but father says I may do just what I please with that wheelbarrow. As soon as I can earn money enough to buy a second-hand wagon I am going to hire the black horse of father and going into the express business. . . . We played leap-frog yesterday, and Will burst out his pantaloons so that he had to go home."

I received the following, with many blots, from Tommy:—

"Friend Robert:

"As I have a few moments to spare and Charlie and Will are writing you, I thought I would write. How do you do? I am well. I am sorry you are sick. What hot wether we do have! My dog is dead — killed. We was afraid he was going to have the hydrarfoby. Did you have to take caster oil? Pils is bad enuf, but that and rubarb is worse. I don't think of no more news now.

"Very Respeckfully Yours,

"Thomas Taylor."

Will sent me a picture of the spelling class, with Cynthia going from the foot to the head, and a wooden contrivance of his own manufacture, labelled "Jumping-Jack." The next I heard from him, Home brought me word that he was down with the fever.

"He says that it's worse than he expected, and he hopes you won't undertake any more such business if you want him for a partner," said Home.

I told Home to tell him the getting well was

pleasant, and I sent him a fancy mould of jelly Mrs. Payson had given me.

Then I kept hearing day after day that he was n't as well, did n't rest well nights, and was delirious; but I was getting on so nicely myself, it did n't occur to me that he could be in danger, until one evening Ed came in to see me, and I noticed that he was very sober. I felt quite lively, but I could n't get him to smile. After he left my room I heard him speaking in a low tone to mother, and heard Will's name mentioned. It flashed across me that Will was dead!

"Mother!" shrieked I.

She came in, looking frightened.

"Mother, is Will dead? Tell me truly, is Will dead?" said I, grasping her arm.

"No, Robbie, he is n't dead," said she, putting her arm around me and drawing me to a chair.

"He 's going to die, then?"

"I hope not."

"But they 're afraid so! They 're afraid so, are n't they, mother?"

She put both her arms around me and pressed

me close up against her. "My boy, Robbie," said she, "it 's all in God's hands."

"Mother, mother," cried I, "I can't have Will die! Why, I can't, mother!"

She only held me the tighter, and kissed my forehead.

"Mother," said I, "call Ed."

Ed had left the house, but he came back. His eyes moistened when he looked at me.

"'T is n't so, is it, Ed?" asked I.

"They 'll do all they can for him, Rob."

"And they won't let him die, you don't think they will, do you, Ed?"

"I don't know, I don't know, Rob dear."

"Can't somebody do something, — can't your father? Why, they must! I can't live without Will."

"Rob dear," said Ed, with a glance towards mother, "we must ask Him who gave us each other to spare us to one another."

I went to him to beg him to have something done. Mother took me away and held me in her arms.

"Rob, my dear Rob, my darling! This is

your first hard lesson. You must learn to wait."

"To wait, mother? To wait for It to come and take Will? How can I wait? Carry me to him, mother! Please carry me to Will!"

"To wait God's will, Rob. We have to learn to be still and wait. He gave you back to me; He will, I think, give Will back to his mother."

She held me closer and closer; and in her arms it seemed, in some way, as if my life was protected, and nothing quite so bad as Will's going out of it could ever happen. She laid her lips on my forehead, and rocked gently until I went to sleep.

When I awoke it was night, the lamp was turned down, and mother lay asleep upon the lounge. Something hard and heavy lay upon my heart; I heard the tick, tick of the little clock in the sitting-room, and it came to me that that something was Will.

I did n't move, for I did n't want to arouse mother; but I lay in the shadows while the clock in the sitting-room ticked, and the lamp, turned down low, made a little singing noise, and the insects out through the open windows chirped, and I thought of Will. I thought of all the plays we 'd played, and all the bright things he 'd said; I thought of all the scrapes he 'd led me into and all the ways he 'd helped me out, and how he 'd never deserted me, and how we had sometimes quarrelled, and always made up, and had always, always loved each other; and the load on my heart grew harder and harder and heavier and heavier.

"Mother," cried I, "mother, may n't I go to the window and put my face against the pane, where last I saw Will's?"

So I went to the window, and there I saw the flash of his eye, I saw his lips twitch, and I saw him toss back that lock that was always falling on his forehead.

Mother drew me away.

"Bring me the notes, the pictures, the wooden images, and all the funny things he has sent me,—*all* of them, mother."

So I lay down holding the things on my bosom. Mother sat in a chair by the bed, and stroked down the side of my forehead.

"You must n't feel so, Rob, you must *not*," said she.

She kept up the movement with her fingers about my temples, and after a little I asked her, "Mother, would it be praying to say, 'Our Father, who art in Heaven, let Will live'?"

"Yes, Rob."

I closed my eyes and said it softly to myself, and the little mantel-clock in the sitting-room and the singing lamp on my table and the chirping insects out at the open window seemed to be saying, "Our Father, our Father, our Father, who art in Heaven, let Will live!"

She kept up the motion with her fingers, and by and by I went to sleep.

In the morning I was worse, but Will was better. Dr. Hammond — dear old doctor! — called to see me, and said that in a fortnight's time he would have Will and I picking chicken-bones together.

I was so happy all that day that I wanted to sing and shout. I played on mother's old accordeon until my arms ached, and Aunt Lovisa said she was crazy.

A fortnight more, and Will had so far improved that I was allowed to call on him. We were so weak that we both laughed and cried when we met. That seemed to set every one else laughing and crying, and we had a very funny time all around.

Homer, who had followed our carriage over, bobbed in, and said we looked like two afternoon shadows.

I did n't make a long call that time, but the next week I went over and stayed all day. Will felt pretty well, and was as full of old Nick as he could hold. We were so weak we had n't either of us a bit of self-control, and when anything particularly funny was said or done we just keeled over on the bed and rolled and giggled

We had our dinner laid out for us on a stand in Will's room, with various dishes that could n't be accommodated on the stand sitting around in adjacent chairs. We got to giggling over something we found in the chicken, and tipped over the stand. Will was afraid the gravy would grease the carpet, and sopped it up with a corner of a bed-blanket. Mrs. Bradley came in, and while she was picking up things I sat down in the chair that had the cranberry sauce in it, and that made dreadful work for me.

After dinner I was sent into the sitting-room to take a nap on the lounge, and Will was put to bed; but I could hear him tossing around, and he had one slat in his bedstead that he kept squeaking, sometimes high, sometimes low. He seemed to be trying to play a tune with it. Then he would spring up and call, "Bob, you awake?" "You got to sleep yet, Bob?" "Don't you smell cranberry sauce, Bob?"

Then he had a turn of rattling the foot-board, and of snoring violently. I had grown a little drowsy when I opened my eyes and saw him standing in the door, his face on a broad grin.

"Here's the sleeping Beauty! Only twenty-five cents admission, gentlemen. He wakes up once in eight-and-forty hours to take his cranberry sauce. Walk up, gentlemen!"

I threw a pillow at him, and he darted away, but that was the last of our nap.

When I went into his room again he wanted

to know how many "wish-bones" I'd saved up; said he had five a-drying, and was going to keep his father buying chickens until he had a dozen.

When I went home he gave me a little wooden pill-box that he said would be nice to keep percussion caps in, a Tale of a Shipwrecked Mariner, and a small bag of cranberries.

We were both sick the next day, but rallied soon, and Will returned my visit. Aunt Lovisa was obliged to leave the house before night.

The week after, I spent two days at Will's house, and he spent two at mine. We rode out together and returned the many calls that had been made upon us. Tommy Taylor, when not otherwise engaged, ran after the carriage, and wherever we stopped he held the gate open and grinned pleasantly. Charlie Payson we frequently saw hard at work with his wheelbarrow. Home was usually about the tin-shop, and seemed to be either unloading or loading up paper-rags. He manifested a deep interest in our diet.

"The strengthening things a fellow has to

take when he 's getting up from a fever are the best part of it," said he.

Our hands and faces skinned, and Will took a diabolical pleasure in peeling them. He peeled himself till he drew blood, and then he attacked me; nothing but a vigorous resistance kept him off. Our hair began to come out, and he expressed the hope that there would n't be a spear of it left.

"How funny we should look with our heads bare! I should want mine shiny, like that bald spot on Dea. Clapp's, and then I should want my ears to stand out straight like Mrs. Taylor's baby's."

I was horrified, but Will brushed and combed, and pulled his hair out by handfuls, until he began to look as if his wishes were to be gratified. Then he complained that his head was cold, and he wanted a flannel night-cap. His mother sewed a piece of red flannel cap shape, and he ornamented it with a wide cotton ruffle, and put it on whenever any of the boys called.

Homer told us frankly that even if we dressed

up our best, we looked like the old Scratch. We had many invitations out, and Will said he should accept them just the same as if he had as much hair as Absalom.

"'T was n't Absalom that had the hair; 't was his brother," said I.

Mrs. Payson invited us to spend a day there, and we fared sumptuously, while all the servants about the establishment were kept running to wait on us. But it seemed to me the house was lined with mirrors, and our ragged faces and thinly-covered heads looked out from all sides of the room.

Mrs. Hammond gave us an entertainment, and there we met among others Cynthia Strong and Sue Vallandigham. They seemed to regard us with a kind of awe.

"At one time I little expected to ever see you again, Will," said Sue, solemnly.

Will bobbed his bare head, and Cynthia eyed him severely.

"I should think that such a sickness must be an awful warning," said she. "The boy that keeps on in his evil course after it must indeed be hardened."

The bare head bobbed again.

Mrs. Taylor invited us over to visit Tommy one afternoon, and though we did n't have much besides hard gingerbread and rhubarb pie, and the baby cried almost all the time, it showed her disposition.

We had plum preserves on the table, and after Tommy had scraped his dish clean he asked me if I was going to leave mine, 'cause if I was he 'd eat it; said his mother did n't often get plum preserves. Tommy's manners are dreadful.

And last of all, who but the master should invite us to dinner! Will said he should n't have been more surprised had he been invited to a seat with a full bench of judges. I thought I should as lief go to jail for a festal dinner as to the master's; but we found Home and Charlie there, and we had a splendid time.

Every one has appeared glad to see us upon the street again and ready to do us a good turn. Even old Capt. Parker, whom we saw in the market selling pears, gave each of us a couple. They were gnarly, to be sure, but I suppose it was as generous for him to give those as it would have been for a different man to give fair ones.

Will says one of the best things about being sick is you find out where some people's good streaks are.

CHAPTER X.

WE MASQUERADE.

WILL and I spent the most of our school vacation out on his grandfather's farm. We had a splendid time, and earned enough at work at haying to pay off the Capt. Parker debt.

The great event we heard most about during vacation was the robbery of the Graceville Bank. The burglars had n't been found when school began.

All the boys were on hand the first day. Charlie had been doing great business with his wheelbarrow during vacation, and had taken on a business air that made him seem about five years my senior.

Homer seemed to feel that he had distinguished himself by having a boil, and talked a great deal about what he "he did for it." He acted kind of proud of it, just as Tommy Taylor's mother does of her baby. Tommy sits with Home, and once Home put up his hand, and said he, "Can't Tom Taylor stop hitting my bile?"

Will was in remarkable high spirits. One of his coat-pockets stuck out more than usual, and he would every once in a while stop studying and clap his hand around upon that pocket as if he was afraid he had lost something. When we were at the blackboard, with our backs to the school, he winked at me and tapped on his pocket, as if there was something pretty interesting there; but Will is always giving me to understand that he has something remarkable in his pockets, so I did n't feel much excited. At recess he gave me another wink and a pinch, and beckoned me around into Martin's shed.

Tommy Taylor, who had seen the wink, tagged on, grinning expectantly; but Will, with half a stick of black licorice, bribed Tom to go back. Then he drew from his pocket and shook before me a false moustache and pair of whiskers!

"Don't be scared," said he. "Are n't they bully?"

"Horrible!" cried I. "Where *did* you get them?"

"Found 'em this morning under a little bridge on the road towards Graceville. Zip chased a chipmunk out there, and I was trying to help him find it. Won't we have some fun with these and the old clothes in your Grandmother Brown's garret?"

"I would n't touch the things for a dollar."

"They 're clean," said he, showing me the wrong side, — as if that was the reason why I was afraid of them!

All the afternoon he kept winking and tapping his pocket, and once he spread his treasures on his atlas under the desk, and was stroking them when the master spoke to him. He came very near being caught. He did n't bring them to school again, but Saturday afternoon he came over to our house early and wanted me to go to Grandma Brown's with him.

Grandma Brown likes small boys, and she said we might play with those clothes in the garret as much as we wished. As soon as we were under the rafters, Will drew out his whiskers.

"I've had dreadful times hiding 'em these last two days," said he. "Nobody knows until he tries it how hard it is to keep anything hid. First I put them under the sofa cushion, and Zip dragged 'em out; then I hid them behind a pile of boxes in the wood-house chamber, and that very day mother set Mrs. Donovan to cleaning that chamber; finally I crowded them into an oyster-can, and hid the can in one of my old rubber boots."

"They don't match your hair, nor eyes, nor anything about you," said I, as he tied them on.

"I don't care for that; some folks' features don't correspond. They make me look ferocious, and that's what I most want." He looked in a piece of broken mirror he had taken from his pocket, and seemed greatly pleased with the reflection. "Now for the clothes! You're to be my wife, you know."

He put on a "butternut" dress suit that had been my grandfather's. It was a mile too large around for him.

"Jerusalem!" said he, "why didn't I eat more dinner? There's a feather cushion in that old rocking-chair,' Rob; toss it over here for stuffing."

Then he had to have another feather cushion on behind, and rags tucked in here and there to fill out, the swallow-tails of his coat pinned up; and after we 'd done our best he did n't look very well proportioned. He tied a scarf over his brown hair, and put a tall gray hat on top.

I dressed up gayly, — in red and blue and green. I had a green silk bonnet with a full ruche and pink roses in the inside. Will said that in the face I had a kind of pollywog appearance, neither boy nor woman, and that I ought to have a veil; so we found a lace veil, which he doubled and pinned over my face.

He gave me his arm, and we started downstairs, but I tripped on my long skirt, and we went to the bottom pell-mell. I never hear grown people say anything about crazy-bones, and I don't know but they "outgrow" them, but crazy-bones make up a large part of a boy. I hit all of mine, and I jammed my bonnet the worst way. Will's cushions broke his fall, and he hopped up and began putting me to rights, and said I "was n't hurt any," which is the way he usually consoles me.

Grandma heard the racket, came up, and forbade our going on to the street, but we finally coaxed her to let us go where Home and Charlie could see us.

"Now," said Will, as we went out, "I shall walk fast and you must come stramming after, and if you could take your dress up on your heels you would appear more natural."

I told him I could n't walk without taking my dress up on my heels.

We first went to the tin-shop. A pedler's cart was before the door, and Home was helping the pedler load up. He paid no attention to us.

"*Warty, waky, sorso bloo, sine tenus pro and pru!*" said Will, stepping up to him.

"I don't care,— don't want to hear your jabber this morning, anyway," said he.

Will began again.

"I know all about it," interrupted Home, motioning us off with one hand while he shoved a lot of baking tins into the cart with the other.

Will opened his mouth and put his finger into it.

"Yes, I see," said Home. "Tremendous cavity there, but I've nothing with which to fill it."

Just then Tommy Taylor came running across to where we were. He thrust his hands in his pantaloons pockets, and stood looking up at us so interested and innocent-like that I turned my head to keep from laughing.

"He's short for his bigness, ain't he, Home?" said Tommy, nodding towards Will.

Will turned towards Tommy and held out his hand. "*Un sou rear vox populi*," said he.

Tommy kicked at him.

"*Un miscreant castigata wir wurza! kla shrink drat shring wurtum!*" shrieked Will, shaking his fists and glaring down at Tommy.

Tommy shrank back against the wall winking hard and looking scared.

"Come now, old fellow," said Homer, brandishing a new quart dipper over Will's head, "take yourself out of the way, or I'll set the dog on you."

Homer's dog is a fierce one, and Will moved on, turning around now and then to shake his fists, and call out something dreadful to the boys. I trotted after, tripping on my long skirts as I went. Without thinking it was wrong, I proposed that we should call at some of the houses and ask for something to eat. Will approved, and we rang the bell of the nearest one. It was Miss Wheeler's, the dress-maker's.

"Please give me a bite, ma'am," said he, when she opened the door.

"No, indeed," said she; "you 're just as well able to work and earn your living as I am." She slammed the door in our faces, and turned the key in the lock.

"There 's that pie, Bridget; you might bring them that," said the mistress of the second house.

The pie looked as if it had been cut a long time. Will thanked her, and tried to take out a piece. The bottom crust was raw and stuck to the plate; the apple was n't cooked, and looked as if sweetened with brown sugar.

"I think I won't take any just now," said

Will, handing it back. "I don't feel as hungry as I did; and my wife, she 's delicate, she can't eat that kind of pie."

"Mabbe you'd be afther havin' me bring on the cake and parserves," said Bridget, grimly.

Will said he thanked her, he did n't care for the cake and preserve, and we left.

"Just come here and look at him, Bridget," called the mistress as we turned down the walk. "His whiskers are too black for his hair, and he 's too short for his whiskers. I believe he 's an impostor!"

"And howly murrther! the woman 's got on man's boots. It 's no woman at all, at all!" shrieked Bridget.

We two boys travelled out of that yard lively. Sheriff Kitely lives opposite, and he was just going into his gate. "By ——!" said he, as he saw us, "if there is n't ——!"

We cut around the corner. "Don't let 's make any more calls," said I, as soon as we dared stop for breath.

"Do for pity's sake draw that scarf up over my hair, and let my coat-tails down a little.

Maybe they 'll make me look taller," said Will.

We rearranged ourselves behind Deacon Clapp's barn, and as soon as we dared, turned back to look up the boys. On High Street we met Rose Payson and Nellie Royce.

"Please give me a penny to buy medicine for my wife. I 'm afraid the poor dear has consumption," said Will, holding out his hand to Rose.

"I sh'd think she 'd go to the hospital, then," said Rose, turning on one foot and looking me over.

"We can't bear to be separated; either of us without the other would pine away, wither up and die," sighed Will.

"Dear me!" said Nellie, diving one hand into her pocket. "I 'm sorry for her. I thought I had a penny, but I can't find it. I read in an almanac the other day about a medicine that would cure consumption. If you only had a dollar you could get that."

I had a coughing spasm.

"Lay your head on my shoulder. There,

dear," said Will, stepping up, and putting his arm around me. "This exertion is too much for her, you see, Miss."

"What a looking bonnet!" said Rose to Nellie, as we moved off.

"Poor thing! I presume she feels so badly she don't care how she looks," said Nellie.

"It's wicked to deceive them so, Will," said I, bobbing my head up from his shoulder.

"Keep quiet!" replied he, rapping me down again. "Here's Doctor Hammond's."

Ed was sitting with his head out at an open front window, and Gustus Hillman was in the yard talking with him.

"Who the Dutch comes here?" said he, as he saw us.

Will began his jabber, but raising his arm, he caught the buttons on his sleeve in his long beard and twitched it to one side.

"Will Bradley," cried Gustus, starting forward, "is that you?"

"I'll bet 't is n't," said Will. And with that we both turned and ran. I tripped on my skirts and fell full length. Ed and Gustus picked me up, and Will came back to inquire if "I'd put my spine out of joint."

Ed hustled us up into his room as if he was afraid of being seen in the street with us, and made us tell our adventures. He and Gustus had lots of fun over us, but said we were out under false pretences and were in bad business, and we had better see Charlie as soon as possible and go home.

I said that if it was a bad business, I would n't take another step in it. But they all said we must go and see Charlie; we must n't back out now. He was working for Mr. Spooner, and we could go that way home.

As we left the house, I had a glimpse of Sheriff Kitely at a window opposite.

CHAPTER XI.

RESULTS OF OUR MASQUERADE.

WE came upon Charlie at the foot of Town Hall Hill. He had just started up the hill with his wheelbarrow.

"Here, bub," began Will, "won't you be kind enough to roll my wife up this hill? She 's delicate, and has just had a prostrate turn."

"Roll your wife up this hill? Of course I shan't," said Charlie.

"Well, she 's got to go up in some way, and you see how feeble she is," said Will, as I lopped on his shoulder.

"I can't help that. 'T is n't my business to carry sick stragglers around the country," replied Charlie, preparing to move on.

"Have n't you any heart, any bowels of compassion?" asked Will.

"Have mercy, sir, have mercy!" groaned I, from behind my veil.

"There! you hear her 'helpless shriek for mercy,'" said Will.

Charlie stopped and looked at us. "Where are you going, anyway?"

"We 're travelling from Boston to Albany for rest and refreshment. We 've been unfortunate, and have nothing with which to hire a carriage."

"There, dear, you must sit down," said Will, tumbling me into the wheelbarrow. "This woman has got to go up this hill,—there 's no other way about it, bub; and either you or I must wheel her up."

"I tell you I shan't do any such thing," said Charlie, growing red in the face.

"Then I must do it myself," said Will, grasping the handles and pushing the wheelbarrow ahead.

Charlie caught him by the swallow-tails. "See here, Mister," said he, "that wheelbarrow belongs to me, and bears my sister's name, and I 'm not going to have you two creatures around with it. If you don't leave in just two seconds I 'll scream "Thieves!" and "Bloody Murder!"

Will's wife scratched out of that wheelbarrow as quickly as she had tumbled in, Charlie trundled off victorious, and Will and I plodded on.

We started home, but as we passed Judge Davis's, the judge, who is one of the overseers of the poor, was in his front door, reading a newspaper, and Will said it would be a good joke to get a pass to the almshouse. Before I could speak he was inside the gate.

"*Weich ann struf berim wrecker* almshouse?" said he.

Judge Davis glanced up at us, and just then Bije Whittlesey, who was working for him, came up for orders.

"Here, Bijah," said he, "take these vagrants to the lock-up, and tell Kitely to keep them shut up over the Sabbath."

We did n't dare say a word, but followed Bije from the yard.

"I think, after all, that we won't go to the alms-house. It 's early yet, and we can travel quite a distance before night," said Will, as soon as we were out of the judge's hearing.

"Wa-al, railly, you 've larned the language of

the country 'mazing quick," said Bije. "It all came to you when you heard the word 'lock-up,' did n't it?"

"Come this way, wifey," said Will, trying to draw me into a side street.

"No, you don't go that way; you don't play any of your little games on me," said Bije, springing in between us, and drawing our arms through his.

"Is n't this a free country?" demanded Will, trying to pull away.

"No, 't is n't; it's under law and officers," said Bije, holding us fast, and marching us along like a couple of criminals.

"You 've no business to pick a man up from the street and shut him into the lock-up," said Will, hanging back.

"I did n't pick you up from the street; and business or no business, Judge Davis's orders are to lock you up. So come along," said Bije, giving Will a twitch forward.

"Well, Mr. Whittlesey," said Will, cheerfully, "what if we 're not vagrants? What if we 're only dressed up to fool folks?"

"Then I sh'd say you deserved to be put in the lock-up more than 's ef you were vagrants," said Bije.

"I *am* Will Bradley, and I won't go another step towards that old lock-up," said Will, stripping off his whiskers and moustache, and bracing himself in the road.

"O Mr. Whittlesey," said I, tearing off my veil, and looking up to him with the full ruche and pink roses around my face, "O Mr. Whittlesey, do let us off!"

"I swaow, if this 'ere ain't little Bob!"

Bije's face broke into a broad grin.

"You will let us off, Mr Whittlesey? We did n't mean any harm; we only did it for fun," said I.

"I don't s'pose *you* did, Bob; but this 'ere Bradley boy is a reg'lar little limb," said Bije, giving Will a shake that tipped his tall hat into the sand and settled his feather cushions a good deal.

"Let me alone!" growled Will. "I want to go home, and I 'll never be caught in such a scrape again."

"That's just what you promised me when you ran away with the capen's team," said Bijah, gripping tightly.

"Oh, please let him off, Mr. Whittlesey! He didn't mean anything wrong. You helped us before, do please help us now."

"I don't know 's 'cording to law I can, if I wanted to ever so bad, Bob. The judge has sentenced you to the lock-up, and I s'pose it's my dooty to see that sentence executed unless he reverses the decision. I s'pose that in the eyes of the law I'm 'sponsible for you."

"Pshaw!" said Will.

"You may pshaw out o' t'other end of your mouth before you're through with it," said Bije, twitching Will up again. "I ain't a-going to lay myself liable by letting *you* off. If little Bob's a mind to take a run at my back, why, I shan't leave you to run after him."

"I shan't leave Will, but I'll run back and ask Judge Davis to 'reverse his decision,'" said I.

"Here's Lawyer Royce in his yard. I'm going to call to him," said Will.

Mr. Royce had seen us, and came down to the gate without being called. I turned my face, surrounded by its full ruche and pink roses, towards him.

"The saints preserve us! What have we here?" cried he.

"It's only I," replied I, humbly.

"So 't is; and this prodigy is my youthful friend, Bradley, is it?"

"Yes, it is," said Will, brightening up. "We're in trouble again."

"I should think likely you might be," said Mr. Royce, punching into the feather cushions. "This is the most singular anatomy I ever met."

"Come here, dear, and take a second look at your poor consumptive and her husband," called he to Nellie, who was peeping out from behind the trees.

I was so mortified I blushed to the roots of my hair, and looked on the ground.

"Well, what are we going to do?" asked Will, crossly.

"Do? I should think you'd done it already.

I should advise you to make tracks for home now, and take off this toggery."

Bije's countenance fell. "Judge Davis ordered me to take um to the lock-up."

"But he supposed we were vagrants; he 'd no idea of shutting *us* up," said Will, jerking away, and being again jerked up by Bije.

"You 're a faithful fellow, Bije; but you 'd better let the boys off this time."

"I shan't be liable to a fine nor nothin', shall I?" asked Bije, letting go his hold on Will a trifle.

"Not a bit of it. You 've done your duty, and I give you my word as a legal adviser that the law shan't touch you."

"Wa-al, just as you say," said Bije. "But I want to say to you, William Bradley, that it 's agin all law and order for you to be cutting around the streets deceivin' folks in this way. And here 's little Bob, who sets his eyes by you, — yer allus gettin' him inter scrapes, and makin' him no eend o' trouble. Yer ought to be ashamed o' yerself."

"Go home now, boys, and don't you ever do it again," said Mr. Royce.

We started off. My dress-skirt was torn nearly off the waist, and my shawl had unpinned. Will's stuffing was badly out of place, and some of it had come out altogether, so that he had to carry it in his arms. I had lost my veil, and Will's whiskers were in his pocket, so that our faces were exposed, and every one who met us knew us.

A shower was coming up, and the wind blew hard. It had been so hot, I had loosened the strings of my bonnet, and all at once there came a gust and whisked it off. It went bobbing along through the air, and skimming over the pavement, and Will and I chased it. Will was ahead, and all at once he disappeared, and sunk beneath the pavement. I was under too much headway to stop, and I, too, dropped, I should say about five hundred feet. I landed in the dark, and on something soft and squirming.

"Jerusalem!" exclaimed the soft pile under me.

"Where *are* we?" cried I.

"We've gone *through* and come out in China. Don't you smell tea?" said Will.

We had fallen into a cellar which was being deepened, and which had an iron trap-door opening on to the sidewalk above. Will had cut his leg on the bit of broken mirror in his pocket, and while we were binding up the wound some one came along on the outside and shut down the door. That did n't frighten us because we knew there were stairs up into the store above, and, though the door at the head of the stairs might be locked, we could rouse some one who would let us out. But it began to rain and Will said we might as well remain where we were until after the shower.

Falling into the soft earth, we had soiled our faces and clothes wretchedly, and we decided that it would be too mortifying to go up through the store. The top of the cellar was a little above the sidewalk, and there were two small windows opening on the inside, through one of which Will thought we could crawl out.

We dragged an empty hogshead up under the window. Will clambered up on to the head, and as soon as the coast outside was clear, he swung back the window and thrust himself part way through, — part way, because when he got as far as the cushions, he was stuck, and could n't move either way. He wriggled his head and shoulders over the sidewalk, and wriggled his heels over the hogshead; but it was no go.

"Confound the *feathers!*" said he; "Bob, you just catch hold of that back cushion and *pull!*"

I was just behind him on the hogshead, and I caught and pulled until all at once the cushion gave way, and I went over backwards a good ways towards China again.

"Thieves, *thieves!*" squeaked a voice coming down the street, a voice I should have known to be Capt. Parker's if I'd landed in Pekin.

"No, 't is n't thieves, either. Hush up!" I heard Will say from outside.

But the people both sides the street had heard, and they all came out. I was up on the hogshead, ready to follow Will out, but the head gave way, and I went down inside; and that hogshead had held molasses.

"This is a female!" said a man who had his head in at the window looking after me.

"Open the door and let her out," said the people on the walk.

That building is n't far from the bank, and the first persons I saw as I came out were my father and that dignified bank president. My father had the funniest wrinkles around his mouth.

"Have you had a good time, Rob?" said he.

"No; I have n't," said I; "I 've had a most miserable time."

"I 'm glad of it," said he; and he never said another word to me about the scrape, — not from that time to this. I more clearly understand what my father means by saying every wrong act brings its own penalty; but when a fellow don't know beforehand that it is a wrong act, it seems to come pretty hard on him.

Will and I ran for home as fast as we could go, everybody laughing at us. Homer said Will left a stream of feathers and I a trail of molasses all the way. Mrs. Donovan found my green silk bonnet, and she wears it now when she goes out washing. I 've never felt like claiming it.

The next Monday afternoon, — a warm, droning kind of an afternoon, when the school seemed to be going to sleep, and Will was getting ready to throw a torpedo on Ike Tucker's desk, — there came a tremendous rap at the door, and when the master opened it there stood Sheriff Kitely.

"William Bradley, if you please, sir," said he.

The room swam and turned dark before me. Will was drawing a picture of Capt. Parker, and he gave the finishing touch to the nose even after that call. Then, when he was half across the school-room, he came back after two golden-sweet apples he had left in his desk.

He went away with the sheriff; and my legs trembled so all the rest of the afternoon I could n't study, and went down three in spelling.

After school, Gustus Hillman said Mr. Royce wanted to question Will about those old whiskers. He said they were the disguise of the Graceville bank robbers, and that Will's and my having them in our possession had made a great deal of talk. Some people thought perhaps my father had been an accomplice of the robbers.

"Being in a bank, he would know all about the vaults and the locks," they said; and Capt. Parker said, "'T was these folks the world thought the most of, and that carried their heads highest, that was at the bottom of the most iniquity."

Tommy asked me if I did n't s'pose if they found out 't was so, they 'd hang my father, and said he should go to see it if they did. Gustus said, "Hush up!" so I did n't know but Gustus thought there was danger of it.

We boys went down to Mr. Royce's office, and he and the sheriff and Will were just starting for the bridge where Will found the disguise. Homer, Tom, and I, and Homer's dog went too.

Will kept telling Sheriff Kitely what his theory of the robbery was, and I slipped around and asked Mr. Royce if anybody really thought my father was an accomplice. "Because," said I, "if they 'll allow me to be a witness, I can testify he was n't!"

"Your father, Rob!" said Mr. Royce. "I should sooner think perhaps it might be a bold and savage man like yourself."

In the bushes near the bridge we found a satchel, fragments of papers, and some gingerbread and cheese. Tommy ate the cheese, and then soaked the gingerbread in the brook and ate that. Home would n't let him feed any of it to the dog for fear it was poisoned.

Mr. Royce thought the papers would enable him to identify the burglars, and I heard my father say they are on the track of them now.

Aunt Lovisa says Will will yet get into a scrape that he won't get out of so easily: she should think Mr. Bradley would expect that boy would ruin him; and she does think my father and mother are just crazy to let me associate with him. Father only smiles, and mother says she thinks she "understands both Will and Robbie." I notice that when mother speaks in that way, Aunt Lovisa don't say much, though she tosses her head a good deal.

CHAPTER XII.

FURTHER EXPLOITS.

WEDNESDAY morning some one woke me up shouting under my chamber window:

"Rob, Rob, they 've got 'em!"

I went to the window in my night-gown, and Will was there terribly excited, with his cap on the back side of his head.

"Put on your pantaloons; don't stop for your jacket!" said he. "They 'll have 'em shut up in the lock-up before we get there! Kitely has only just come. They 'd got most to Canada before he caught them."

Then I knew he meant the burglars. I did n't stop to wash or comb my hair. We had n't had breakfast, but Aunt Lovisa was n't around, and mother gave me five buttered griddle-cakes to take in my hand.

Judge Davis had kept the lock-up key while Mr. Kitely was gone, so they had to send to the

Judge's after it, and the burglars were on that wooden bench on the hotel piazza. Homer and Charlie and Tommy had got there, and Homer's dog; and Tommy has got a pup, and that was there too.

One of the men was very handsome; he had the reddest whiskers I ever saw. The other had a very red face and was quite good-looking. They had both tried to get away, and both had on fetters; and the handsome one wore hand-cuffs.

It was a very chilly morning, and some one called to Mr. Kitely to come into the bar-room and "have a cup of coffee." Almost all the men went into the bar-room after coffee and left us boys to guard the robbers. I did n't care to go very near, and Charlie is too polite, so we stood back a little; but Will is n't a very polite boy; he did n't wait for any introduction, but just stepped up and went to talking. Says he confidentially, —

"Could you keep any of the money away from Kitely?" Had n't I known Will I should have thought he rather hoped they had.

They did n't answer.

"You did n't expect they 'd get you, did you?"

"Ain't you sorry you did it, now?" asked Tommy, putting his nose right up in the red-faced man's face.

"I bite," said the red-faced man.

Tom darted back at that, and pitched off the piazza backward into a flower-bed.

Both the burglars laughed, and their laugh sounded just as natural, just as any man's would.

Charlie and I stepped up a little nearer.

Will was down on his knees examining the fetters on the red-faced man's ankles.

"This must be a darn mean county if the sheriff can't show a handsomer set of anklets than those," said the man.

"All out of style, are they?" asked Home.

"Kitely never did keep up with the fashions," said Will, as if he was a good deal mortified. "How do they go on and off, though?"

"Why," said the man, "they 're just the simplest thing. The sheriff has the key; but you see that little hole. You might pry that little hasp back with almost anything."

"That's so," said Will. "I wish I had something to try it."

"Well," said the man, "you just come here and put your finger in my upper vest-pocket; you'll find a little narrow steel bar that I believe would open that."

Will found the little bar, and we boys came up and sat down on the piazza floor around the man's feet, to see if the hasp could be pried back. The man told him how, and after a little he pushed just right and the lock slipped back. Will knew too much to take off the fetters: he just wanted to see if you could open them without the key; but the minute that burglar saw the bar worked, he just sprang off the bench, hitting some of us on the head with his boot-heels, and before we had the least notion what was going on, he was off the piazza.

Will clutched at his coat, but did n't get it. We shouted, "Stop thief, stop thief!" and ran after him, shouting, "Stop, stop!" but he would n't.

The dogs barked and ran; the men coming

out of the bar-room yelled, "Where is he?" and Bijah Whittlesey, coming with the lock-up key, stood in the street with his mouth wide open until he shut it to say, —

"That Bradley boy is the darndest little cuss!"

Kitely sprang on his horse and dashed down past us, and we boys dashed after him, and all the men about the hotel dashed after us. We could see the burglar's brown coat far ahead of us all.

Mr. Kitely chased him nearly to the Grew woods, and there he lost sight of him. A part of the men went around the woods, and a part came back with us boys to lock up the other burglar.

The other burglar was gone! — utterly disappeared. It did n't seem possible.

"Jerusalem!" said Will, "what's going to be done now?"

Tommy went up and put his finger on a spot on the bench, and said he, —

"When we left, he sot right there!"

Home looked around to see if there was a

hole anywhere through which he could have crawled under the piazza floor.

The men who had come back swore a good deal at everybody. My mother does n't wish me to hear such language, and I went with Charlie and looked up a pear-tree to see if the burglar had climbed up there.

The building opposite the hotel is the school-house, and the only two women who were up in the hotel had been in the kitchen, so no one had seen where he went.

I was afraid to go home alone, so Will went with me. He said he should n't go to school until that burglar was found; said that since he had been the means of letting him go, he felt that he *ought* to stay and help hunt him up.

Homer stayed out, and Tommy ran away at recess. The greatest excitement was over the last man. The girls thought he must have committed suicide, till Ike asked them what they supposed had become of the remains. At recess we all went over and looked at the bench where he last was seen. I sat down on it.

At about three o'clock in the afternoon a noise

was heard in the street, and a boy who sits by the window made such motions that we all stretched our necks, and those of us who are small partly rose to look out.

"Order!" said the master, and we all sank down.

The sounds came nearer and we all looked up again.

"Order!" said the master, and we all sank down.

The boy by the window made most exciting gestures. Then said the master, —

"The first boy I see looking out again, I shall ferule."

"May I be excused?" said Gustus Hillman.

"No, sir."

"May I g'wout?" said Ike Tucker.

"No, sir."

"May I step to the door just a minute, please?" said Charlie Payson.

"No, sir; the next boy that asks me to go out I shall keep in at recess to-morrow morning."

"Please, sir, they've got the burglar. Can't

school close at ten minutes before four to-night?" said I.

"No, sir. Let me see you give your attention to your book."

Pretty soon the door opened, and Will, Homer, and Tommy all filed in. They looked perfectly happy, and it made us realize how much we 'd lost.

The Master called those "three young gentlemen" to his desk to account for being absent, and they all said they 'd had permission from their fathers and would bring notes so stating to-morrow morning.

Will asked to speak but he could n't get permission. After school, though, he perched himself upon a desk and Home on one opposite, while we boys gathered around, and they told us about the capture.

"They found him in Mr. Strong's barn, and it 'll be quite a feather in your cap, Cynthia," said Home.

"They drove him out of the woods, you see," said Will, "and they all thought he went in an opposite direction from the barn, but

Capt. Parker had a glimpse of him skirting through the bushes in the pasture, and we surrounded the barn, but while the men went up after him he knocked a board off the outside and jumped down from the side they did n't expect."

"They'd left no one but us boys to guard that side, because they did n't see how he could get out that way, and he'd got off again had n't Will just grabbed him by the legs and held him," said Home.

We all looked admiringly at Will; he seemed quite modest.

"He just pounded Will with his fists; but you held like a good one, did n't you, Will?" said Tommy.

Just then the board over the ventilator fell as if it had been accidentally knocked down.

Our school-room is in the second story of the building, and there's an opening into the attic, with something like a trap-door which we can pull up or lower by a rope.

"I'd like to know what made that fall," said Ike.

He drew it up again, and it came up easily as usual, and we concluded the children in going from the lower school-room had jarred it down.

We stopped to play ball on the green, and Will threw the ball so that it went through the attic window. There are two windows exactly facing each other in that attic, and while we stood looking at the broken pane, I thought I saw something moving between them. Will grasped my arm.

"There 's some one up there; it 's that burglar!"

We did n't see anything more, and Home said it had all been a notion, but Will said it was n't a notion, and left us boys to watch the house while he went for Mr. Kitely.

Mr. Kitely came with three other men, and the school-house key. Two of the men stayed at the outside door, and Mr. Kitely and the other man and we boys went up into the school-room. They put a ladder up to the ventilator, and Mr. Kitely took his pistol out, and went up the ladder, and put his head through the ventilator.

It was a thrilling moment, but instead of a commotion up there, Kitely just stepped down on the next ladder round and looked down on us, and said he, —

"I'll give you *Jessy*, young Bradley, for trumping up this sell."

"He *was* there!" said both Will and I.

"—— some beam they saw," said one man.

"Does a beam have a head, and dodge out of sight?" said Will.

"When we left school that ventilator was open, and when we came in here the board was down," said Home.

We all remembered Ike's having opened it. I was so sure the man was somewhere in the house that I ran out-of-doors.

Mr. Kitely finally decided to search the building, and they found the man in the cellar behind the furnace. Will told him how we happened to discover him, and seemed surprised that he did n't appear to enjoy the joke better; and Tommy asked him if he was n't ashamed to "make all this fuss."

Mr. Bradley took both the burglars to

Worcester, to lodge them in the jail, and we boys went to the depot with them. Will asked if he could n't have enough of the "reward" to treat us boys with chocolate mice or something, but no one paid any attention to him.

I was glad we were through with the burglars, for Will and I seemed to have been unpleasantly mixed up with them.

The next Wednesday Will was not in school at either session, and as soon as we were dismissed I ran down to look him up. He was sitting in the front door, and his face was swollen and tied up with a handkerchief. He smelled of hops and paregoric, and said he 'd had the toothache. He was gloomy, and said he did wish something would turn up; he was tired of this sameness of things.

"I 'm sure there has n't been much sameness; there were the burglars," said I.

"Pho! what were the burglars?" said he, contemptuously.

"I wish that mountain over there would break forth into fire, smoke, and melting lava," said he. "I should enjoy the excitement,—smoke, hot water, and ashes a-flying, streams of fire hissing down the mountain, and people running with their silver teapots and money bags, just as they did years ago over there in Pompey."

"Not *Pompey*," said I.

"Hercules, then; I would n't be particular which one. I should want everybody to get away safely; and then what fun it would be to come back the next morning, walk over the roofs of the houses, and see a chimney or a church steeple sticking out here and there. What good times we should have in digging down to our things! If I lived anywhere around in Italy I should go to Hercules; but now I should have to cross the ocean, and I a'most know I should fall from the ship's mast-head and be drowned. I wish I could go somewhere, though; I've never been beyond York State. What's York State?"

I replied that York State was a great deal, and tried to show Will that it was.

"Pho! there are the Rocky Mountains and the Sandwich Islands, Hindostan and Cape Good-Hope; don't talk to me of Yor-rk State!"

"There 's going to be a Sabbath-school picnic next week," said I, thinking best to divert his mind.

"I don't care anything about picnics; they 're too tame. I 've been reading about a boy who robbed a melon patch. I 'd like to rob a melon patch; but all the melons around here are gone-to-seed cucumbers, and I might steal enough to kill myself and nobody would make a fuss about it."

I had heard my father read something from the newspaper about "dangerous characters," and the horrible thought flashed across me that Will talked like a "dangerous character."

"Let 's go down to the depot and ramble around among the engines," said he, getting up and knocking the paregoric, peppermint, and camphor bottles on the floor into one heap.

I hinted that his face was too much swollen to warrant his appearing on the street; but he did n't mind what I said, and we went on to the depot.

When we reached the depot there were engines and a freight train in, cars were being switched off and backed up, trains running through, and a great deal going on. Will always wants to be in the midst of things, and we went out among the tracks and around the turn-table.

"Look at the lettering on those cars," said he, as a long freight train rushed past. "'Through Freight, Atlantic to the Pacific, — Blue Line, — San Francisco, Omaha, St. Louis, Chicago, New York, and Boston.' How much and how far they travel! — going all the time; and here are we just stuck down still in this place, Baywater, Baywater, *Baywater* on all sides of us!"

"Look out, there!" shrieked voices back of us. A man twitched Will off the track, and an engine shot by like lightning.

Will just stood and stared at the track. I thought I should faint. We finally went over and sat down on the freight-house platform, and Will dropped his head in his hands. The workmen were talking.

"That was a mighty narrer escape," said one.

"If he had n't been snatched off that instant 't would a-took him," said another.

"I wonder there ain't more of 'em run over than there is. They 're daown araound here all hours of the day, and the carelessest set of young ones in the country."

"Learn you a lesson about hangin' around depots, won't it, bub?" said one to Will.

Will did n't answer, but crossed over the track and started for home. He had n't spōken since he was pulled off.

"It was dreadful, was n't it, Will?" said I.

He lifted up his face, and he was white as a ghost.

"Where should I have been now, Bob?" asked he.

Of course, I could n't very well answer, but it sent cold chills over me. No more was said, and Will turned in at his own gate while I went on.

Will was at school the next day, but he was sober, and did n't appear to take an interest in anything. At recess I managed to get him out on one side the yard alone with me.

"What *is* the matter, Will?" said I; "you don't act at all like yourself."

"Don't want to," growled he. "I 'm sick of

myself, Bob; I 'd be glad enough to be somebody else if I could. Everybody is disgusted with me. I 'm a disgrace to my parents and 'a stumbling-block and a rock of offence' in this school; I 'm an evil associate for you, and have led you into the 'ways of iniquity' time and again. I 'm never going to play with you any more."

I laughed out,—what Aunt Lovisa calls my "nervous laugh."

"Giggle, will you? I don't feel much like giggling. I 've come near dying, and near being killed, besides a good many accidents, within the past three months; and I believe it 's time I began to take advice and behave myself. I would really like to be good,—good as Ed is, you know; but I don't s'pose I ever shall."

The bell rang just then, and I never was more glad to hear it. I could n't bear to hear Will talk so solemn.

Something happened that afternoon for which I was very sorry. Sue Vallandigham expects to be a poetess, and she practises a good deal nowadays. She don't like Will, but she 's written a great deal of poetry at me. The master that afternoon saw her passing a spelling-book to my desk, and made her read the paper that was in it. This was it,—

Thou art not like the run of boys,
O Robert!
There is a gentleness and a winsomeness in thee
That disarms criticism.
Thou art not like those rude boys with whom
Thy lot is cast, but seemst to walk apart;
And in thy blue eyes I see reflected the light
Of far-off worlds.
Since thou hadst that scarlet fever,—fearful disease!—
Thou hast been pale, puny, peaked, of ethereal mould,
As if thy body couldst not hold thy soul;
And sometimes I sit and think, when the sunshine
Shines on the floor,—
How shouldst we miss thy innocent prattle,
And one boy who would not tattle;
Who did not carry gunpowder and bumblebees
And rubber snappers, in his pocket;
Who was kind alike to rich and poor,
And had good lessons.
I hope thou willst break away from bad influences;
Scorn the tempter and his folly,
Though he be both smart and jolly.
He will work you only ill,
Just so sure as his name is Will.

The reference to bad influences made Will bluer than ever, and the poem did n't make me feel very comfortable. I asked mother that night if she thought I needed anything "strengthening."

All the next morning Will was very absent-minded, studying a lesson we 'd taken three days before, and when asked why, in computing interest at six per cent, we reckon five mills for every odd day, replying, "For Bob's sake." Just before intermission he brightened up a little; and as I left the yard for home he came up and ran his arm through mine, and says he,

"I 'm going to do it, Bob."

"Going to do what?"

"Going to turn over a new leaf, fair and square; no backing out allowed."

"O Will, I would n't!"

"*Would n't!* Why not?" asked he, stopping and looking astonished and disappointed.

"I don't want you to try anything new: you 'll get into some scrape or other. I think it 's safer for you to keep right along as you are."

"Oh! but Bob," said he, putting his arm

around my shoulders and giving me a squeeze, "I 'm going to be a better boy; I 'm going to remember that there 's somebody in the world besides Will Bradley; I 'm going to try more to please my father and mother and the master. That is n't all, either: I 'm going to the root of the matter, — I 'm going to try under all my doings to *be* better."

"If you really do that, I think it will be a great improvement, Will," said I.

"Give us your hand on it, Bobby."

"The only thing I 'm afraid of," added he, "is that I shall get discouraged and back out. I 've had two or three such spells before."

"If I was in your place I 'd tell Ed; he understands all about such things, and maybe he could help you," said I.

Will declared that was a good idea, and at the next recess we held an interview with Ed, back of Martin's shed.

"If you honestly wish to be a better boy, Will," said he, "there 's nothing in the world to prevent, — no secret or mystery about it. None of us are very good; but some of us work towards it and some of us don't, and that makes a difference. When you know what is right, *do* it; and when you don't know, try to find out."

"Supposing I try it three or four weeks, and then comes a week when I get careless, don't ask whether an act is right or wrong, and should n't care if I did ask? After that I 'm discouraged, and feel that it 's no use trying."

"Oh! you must n't do that way. You *must n't* give up," said Ed.

I crept away. I can't bear to hear serious talk, it makes me feel so kind of queer. I hope it is n't because I 'm so wicked.

But Will has been a better boy. Homer says "something has come over him," and Cynthia and Sue say they "hope it will last a while." He has n't done anything remarkably good, but he, himself, seems different; he 's more thoughtful about injuring people's feelings; he does n't draw pictures, nor make deaf-and-dumb letters in school; and he blacks his father's boots, brings in wood for his mother, and runs on errands, without making a fuss about it.

CHAPTER XIII.

IN THE WOODS.

THE week after Will turned over his new leaf we had a Sabbath-school picnic in the Grew woods. We usually have our picnic in June; but at that time this year the superintendent was sick, and it was deferred.

We played in a gorge back of the woods, where none of the grown people came. The girls ornamented themselves with leaves and flowers to represent the seasons. Rose, with red and yellow leaves and scarlet berries, was autumn; Hattie Davis, with green leaves and grasses, was summer; Nellie said she would play that blue gentians and golden-rods were violets and apple-blossoms, and dress for spring. Ed told her she was a spring flower herself. I think it is silly for a boy like Ed to talk nonsense to a little girl like Nellie. Why don't he take one of his own age? Will said he himself was going to be stern old winter, and rigged himself out with hemlock sprigs and strips of birch bark in a wintry and ghastly manner.

When we were putting our lunch on the table, Charlie Payson opened a tin pail Sue Vallandigham had brought, and there were three dreadful dried-apple pies! Charlie clapped on the cover again.

"Keep quiet, Bobby," whispered he.

But when we sat down, and Sue saw that the pies were n't on the table, she pushed back her chair, dove under the table and brought out the pail. Will, who was sitting beside Rose, gave me a glance out of the corner of one eye, but he went on talking, and none of us appeared to observe it, — that is none of us but Tommy, — when Sue crowded her three pies on the table. Tommy said, —

"You don't catch me with those!"

Tommy ate of everything good, like a little raven; and I don't believe he brought a thing. Ed and Will, out of regard to Sue's feelings, each took a piece of pie; but, when she was looking the other way, Will threw his under the table.

After supper we played in the woods, told conundrums and fortunes on the ferns; then there came up a shower and we had to take refuge under the table. Will sat down on the piece of Sue's pie he had thrown there, and we had a very funny time. Ike Tucker, who came stalking around in an aimless kind of a way, crawled under the table for shelter, and told us a story about how when he lived up in Vermont, he once went raccoon-hunting. Will became very much interested, and declared that on the first moonlight night we boys must go 'coon hunting in the Grew woods.

The next day he talked 'coon-hunt all the time. He was performing an example on the blackboard and wanted the eraser, and he asked for "the raccoon." The large boys scoffed about equally at Will and at his 'coon. Harry Blakeslee, a young man in our school who wears a mustache and perfumes his handkerchief, inquired why, while we were about it, we did n't hunt grizzlies in the Grew woods? But Ike, who is always ready for fun, and who professes to be an experienced hunter, volunteered to take charge of a party of us.

We had the most exciting times in getting our fire-arms ready. Charlie Payson brought to school his father's seven-shooter, silver-mounted, to ask Ike if that "would do"; Homer tore around until he found a gun that sometimes failed to go off, but when it did go never failed to "kick," then he invested his entire capital in three different kinds of shot, and forgot that he needed powder and caps; I spent all my leisure time in burnishing up an old musket I had found in grandpa's garret; Will melted lead pipe and cast bullets day and night; and Tommy Taylor, who had neither arms, ammunition, nor money, and whose father had expressly forbidden his going, talked largely of how "that 'coon" would feel when he saw us a-coming.

Will undertook training Zip by half-starving him, because he thought a hungry dog would hunt best; but he kept him a little too short, for Zip broke away and stole the family beefsteak.

A difference of opinion arose as to how we should dress, — some said we ought to have shooting-jackets; some said rubber overcoats were the thing. Ike said it did n't matter, the 'coon was n't as sagacious an animal as the fox, and was n't as particular about what people wore hunting.

My mother had objected to my going, but my father gave his consent, charging Ike to take care of me, and bring me back before ten o'clock. He would n't allow me to carry the musket.

When, after tea, we met at Will's we were all heavily accoutred, and Charlie had gotten himself up elegantly in a suit his father wore fox-hunting when he was in Rome. Mrs. Bradley gave us a great many cautions, and took away nearly all our powder. We were just ready to start when the question arose as to how a raccoon looked. How should we know him when we met him? All we could learn from Ike was that he looked like a woodchuck, except that he had a striped tail.

"Except that he has a striped tail, — has a

striped tail," muttered Home to himself, as if he was learning geography.

Will found raccoon in Webster's pictorial dictionary, and we studied the picture until we could see how it looked with our eyes shut. (The face of the raccoon in the dictionary looks some like Tommy Taylor.)

We were in the edge of the woods when we heard something running and panting after us. Home thought maybe it was the 'coon, and he stepped forward so as to bring Ike and I between himself and the animal.

The animal proved to be Tommy Taylor. He had heard something about rubber overcoats, and had come in his father's. It flapped around his legs like a blanket.

"I thought your father forbade your coming," said Will.

"Did," chuckled Tommy; "but I went to bed early, and came down on the wood-shed roof."

Will was for sending him home, but Tom would n't be sent home, and followed on sulkily.

The dogs did n't appear exactly as we had

expected. They smelled around Tommy a good deal, but did n't start on the trail of any other game.

"Let 's sit down and eat our lunch, and give them time," said Home.

Home is the greatest boy for lunches; wherever we 're going he proposes taking one. Then he always forgets his own, and has to eat with Will and Charlie, who usually bring something good. After we had eaten, Ike said we must separate, and go into different parts of the woods, so as to have a better chance for starting up the game.

"No," said Home, "we ought not to break the strength of the party."

But Ike insisted, and sent the boys off in different directions. I remained with him, as my father had directed. After we were left alone, he sat down on an old log, and had a long laugh all to himself.

"Ike," said I, "I don't believe you think there 's any raccoon here."

"Supposing there is n't?" Half the people in the world are hunting 'coons where there are n't any; but so long as they believe there are, they enjoy the hunt just as well."

We had n't been there long before we heard Tommy scream, "Ike, Ike, *Ike!*" and he came crashing through the underbrush, tripping up on his long coat, and tearing himself shockingly. He had seen the 'coon!

"Awfullest looking creature!" gasped he. "Large as a sheep, snarled and spit and hissed — chased me half-way back — thought 't would get me — don't catch me alone again!"

Just then we heard the report of a gun, and we started in the direction of the firing, Tom and I keeping close behind Ike. We found Home lying on his back in a blackberry thicket; he had fired his gun. He had seen the animal.

"'T was n't any 'coon; 't was large as a calf — crouched down, creeping along under those bushes. When it heard me, it turned its head — eyes looked like balls of fire. Oh! I never — saw — anything like it!"

Home trembled like a leaf, Ike was a good deal excited, and I never was so frightened in my life. I expected something would spring out from the bushes or down from the trees, and fasten its claws in me. Tom cried and wished he had n't come.

Ike plunged through the bushes in the direction Home said the animal had taken, and we boys followed because we did n't dare stay behind. Home claimed great credit for his courage in firing, and talked as if the animal, wherever it was, was suffering from its death wound. We came into a space of open woodland.

"*There he is — there — fire, Ike, fire!*" cried Home, dodging behind Ike.

Tom and I caught Ike around the waist. It was dreadful there in the night, in the heart of the woods, with unknown animals with eyes of fire on all sides of us.

"Hold on, boys; it's only me," said the strange animal in a voice like Will's.

Oh! how relieved we were to find it was not a raccoon!

Will had neither seen or heard the animal, had lost Zip, and was a good deal discouraged. Just then Homer's dog was heard barking as if he had found game, and we dashed ahead.

We found Leo at the foot of a large maple. He had treed the game.

The excitement was now tremendous. Tom and I concluded to stop where we were; the other boys cautiously approached the tree. Ike cried out that he saw the animal crouched on a branch. Home pronounced it a panther. Ike, Will, and Home took up line together, and fired. Will's rifle missed; Homer's kicked him over, as usual; Ike brought down the game.

We all rushed up.

It was a great yellow house-cat!

"*Golly!*" said Home at length.

Will went up and poked the "animal" over with the butt of his gun.

"It 's Mrs. Deacon Clapp's cat, boys," said he; "and I would n't have had it killed for five dollars. She just worshipped that cat!"

That made us feel rather gloomy, for Mrs. Deacon Clapp is one of our best friends Will picked up the cat, which he said Mrs. Clapp might like to stuff and keep *in memoriam;* and we went to look up Charlie. After a good deal of shouting, and hunting, and some fright, we found him sitting on a bowlder in the pasture east of the woods. He had lost himself, had waded through the marsh, torn his gay shooting-jacket, ruined his trousers, and lost his cap.

"I tell you, boys," said he, "if a man is going to hunt with any comfort, he wants open land, and a horse to do it on. Woods are no place to hunt in!"

It was useless thinking to find the things we had lost that night, and we went directly home, — Will with the yellow cat thrown over his shoulder. Zip was lost entirely.

CHAPTER XIV.

CATS, DOGS, ETC.

IKE went out early the next morning and hunted up the caps, coats, and guns we had lost, but could n't find Zip. Tommy Taylor came to school looking very subdued, and he frequently heaved a sigh, especially when he sat down suddenly. Will, who lacks delicacy of feeling, asked him what happened between himself and his father that morning, and he said, "Oh! nothin'," and spat on his slate.

Will and I carried the yellow cat down to Deacon Clapp's. We had dreaded it the worst way, and had planned how to break the news to the old lady gently.

"We must leave the cat outside, and go in looking very sober," said Will. "After a while, I shall say, 'How long since you 've seen your cat, Mrs. Clapp?' and when she says, 'Not since last night,' I shall draw a sigh, — you draw one too, Bob, — and I shall say, 'You 've seen her alive for the last time, I fear, Mrs. Clapp.'"

But when Mrs. Clapp's housemaid ushered us into the sitting-room, there on her velvet cushion lay the very cat we supposed we had left at the door.

"Why, where — where did *she* come from?" gasped Will.

"Betty? why I've had her these fifteen years, — you know Betty, Will."

"Why," said Will, in a burst of joy, "I thought we shot her!"

After we 'd explained matters, we buried the strange cat in the river without ceremony. I suppose her relatives came to the funeral, for while we were playing leap-frog before afternoon session, Rose and Nellie, who had been playing down by the river, came running up greatly agitated, and said there was a poor little kitty swimming down the river on a board, and if some one did n't get it out quick, it would drown.

Will came near drowning himself, but rescued the kitten, and handed it to Rose.

It was a poor, homely, draggled, half-starved little thing, and so cold and frightened it trembled like a leaf; but Rose wiped it dry on her silk apron, and held it to her neck until it warmed up. She and Nellie took turns in fondling it, and kissed its little blue nose as much as if it had been a beauty. We named it Moses. When the bell rang, Rose pinned her handkerchief around it to keep it warm, and put it under her desk. While she was out reciting, it tumbled out of the desk and crawled on to the floor. The handkerchief was pinned tightly around its body, and when it tried to walk, the pins stuck into it, and it stood there mewing, its little yellow tail erect, trembling and a-trembling.

The master said whoever that cat belonged to might raise his hand.

Rose owned it, and the master sent her out with it. She shut it up in Martin's shed. At boy's recess, Tommy Taylor slyed off into the shed, and by and by we heard a kitten's wailing from that direction. We went up on tiptoe, and looking in, saw Tommy with both hands around the kitten's throat, squeezing it and giggling over it.

Will went softly in, caught Tommy by the back of the neck, and gave him just such a choking as he was giving the kitten.

"I — I — I only wanted to see its eyes b-b-bung out," blubbered Tommy.

"That's just as I felt about your eyes," said Will.

"If there's anything in this world contemptibly cruel and cowardly, it is tormenting dumb animals," said Ed Hammond.

"That's so, Ed," said Will, savagely glaring at Tommy.

"He ought to be strung up; that's just what ought to be done with him," said Home, who always comes in strong on the popular side.

We agreed that we would n't speak to Tommy again until that time the next day. We wrote a note to Rose, telling her how her kitten had been treated, and advising her to put it in a safer place; and we pinned the note on the shed door where she could n't fail to see it when she came out.

She and Nellie privately carried the kitten into the dressing-room, put it into Almina Harris's dinner-pail where were some crumbs they thought "it could live upon," crowded down the cover, and set the pail away on the upper shelf. When they went after the kitten at night, it was dead as a door-nail. They both lifted up their voices and wept. Tommy Taylor was triumphant, danced a schottische, and would n't be put down; Almina was indignant, and sputtered about the way they 'd used her pail; and we had dreadful times all round.

Charlie Payson wanted a funeral, and offered his watered white envelope-box for the use of the mourners. The box was too long and too shallow, but by spreading the kitten out and tying the cover on it did very well. We dug a grave with shingles we tore off the shed. Homer is such a lazy boy he can't even be one of four to dig a kitten's grave without giving up before he gets it deep enough. We lowered the box by means of ribbons Rose had ripped off her apron.

Charlie Payson thought it belonged to him to

pronounce the eulogy because he had proposed having the funeral. Will thought it belonged to him, because he had saved the subject from the river. Neither of them would give up, and for a while we had two eulogies going on at the same time; but Will has the best command of language, and out-talked Charlie.

We filled up the grave, and Will planted in the fresh earth a bean,—the last of his spring-gun ammunition. "It'll come up nice and viny, you see, Rose, and you can play it's an ivy," said he.

Of two shingles we made a head-board in the form of a cross, and Gustus Hillman gave us a Latin motto to chalk on it. The motto was, "*Requies-cat.*"

"Means, in English, 'Gone to be an angel,'" said he.

"Then 'tis n't true, and I'm not going to have any falsehoods on my monuments," said Rose.

Then Gustus said foreign languages admitted of a variety of renderings. This, if she preferred, might be translated, "Thou reposest, O Cat!"

She said she did prefer; and we had the Latin in white chalk on the front side, and the English in red on the back.

The next morning Sue Vallandigham brought Rŏse the following

LINES ON A DEPARTED KITTEN.

To R. M. P. from S. A. V.

An innocent kitten fell into the river,
  Its cries the air did rend:
A young girl did it discover,
  And feared its life must soon end.

She called a friendly boy;
  He waded in and got it out.
It was a pretty toy;
  Its tail three inches long, — about.

Its color was yellow,
  Its eyes a mild blue;
It was choked by a fellow,
  Who made it mew.

All that could be was done its life to save;
  But it died in a dinner-pail,
And was buried in the darksome grave,
  While we all did wail.

O beauteous kitten, fare thee well!
Green grows the grass above thy tomb.
How our hearts ache none can tell:
Thou art gone in thy youthful bloom.
Farewell!

Will mourned for Zip for two days, and then he seemed to recover spirits, and invited our class in arithmetic up to his house to spend the evening and cipher together. We're in partial payments in arithmetic, and I don't know as we shall ever get out.

By having the master tell us what to do, the large boys to help us do it, and by ciphering together, we've floundered through two or three of those examples, but it's exhausting. When Will is in the mire, of course I'm down by his side, and when he's on dry land, I'm there too. He every morning comes to school, fresh and hopeful, takes out his slate and Arithmetic, sets down the principle, and spiritedly computes the interest to the time the first payment was made; but in less than fifteen minutes his work is so muddled up that it takes the master, Ed Hammond, and Ike Tucker, all three, to pick it out, and start him on again.

Homer has even worse times. He makes such big sprawly figures that he can't put an entire example on his slate, and by the time he gets to the end, the first part is rubbed out, and if he's made a mistake on the way, it is all over with him.

Charlie is the best mathematician in the class. He keeps his work distinct, and always knows whereabouts in an example he is, which must be one great comfort.

The girls take turns in weeping. We have one or more of them shedding tears in recitation every day, and they weep at irregular intervals all the time. Nellie Royce is particularly cast down.

"Robby," said she tearfully the other night, "I don't know anything and I never shall, and I shall mortify my father to death." With that she cried worse than ever.

Cynthia is sullen, but if she once gets hold of anything, she sticks and hangs like a little wood-tick, until she gnaws her way through. The master don't approve of our ciphering together: he says it isn't a self-reliant way; but Will says, "Hang self-reliance while you are in partial payments!" And we decided to hang it, and went to Mr. Bradley's.

Every one was hopeful. Home had bought a new slate half as large as the blackboard; we had all laid in bountifully for slate pencils, and dulled all the jackknives in the company in sharpening them. The dining-room was given up for our use and we ranged ourselves about the table, — the boys around Charlie, the girls around Cynthia.

With a good deal of trouble and many explanations from our leaders, we went through the first example; but though our answers agreed with each other, they did-n't agree with the book. Will thought "the book must be wrong," but Charlie discovered that we had computed it at six per cent, when it should have been seven. Homer wanted to know if we could n't *add in* the seven per cent.

"Let's let it go," said Will; "if a man is so hard up as to have to make such little dabbing, scattering payments, I say let's give him the difference between six and seven per cent. I'm going to bring on the refreshments."

With that he disappeared into the darkness of the pantry. We heard him knocking around among the glassware, tipping over a tin dish or two, and finally putting his head in through the sitting-room door, and screaming, "Mother, mother, where did you set 'em?"

Then he bobbed back into the darkness again, and presently we heard a slopping and a splashing sound, a tin pan clattered off on the floor, and Will appeared in the door, dripping with milk.

"Jerusalem!" gasped he.

Then Mrs. Bradley came upon the scene, and there was much sopping up, wiping and sponging, and some scolding. In the midst of it there came a scratching and a low whining at the door. Will threw it open, and in bounded Zip.

He licked Will's face all over, ran around the room, barked, and wagged, and yelped, tipped over the apple-dish, and narrowly missed the lamp. Mr. Bradley, when he came from the store, told us that Zip had appeared at Will's Grandfather Goodrich's the night after the hunt, much the worse for wear; but Grandma Goodrich had nursed him up, and grandpa brought him down to the store.

Charlie and Cynthia, who had continued at work upon the example, brought the answer out right; and after we had copied their operation, Will took Zip in his arms, and we sat around the fire, and ate apples and grapes, and told bear and ghost stories of a thrilling, hair-starting character. Will was particularly dreadful with the tale of a "headless horseman." When the clock struck nine, we all started as if the ghosts had spoken.

On his way home Homer thought he caught a glimpse of Will's "headless horseman," started to run, tripped and fell, bruising his face so badly that his expression of countenance for the next few days was far from pleasing.

The remainder of our term passed off pleasantly, but with nothing notable happening. We had chestnutting excursions, and political demonstrations, and a menagerie came to town. Will tried hard to be a good boy, though he once in a while made what he called "a bad back-slide." The fortnight before the close of school the large scholars were engaged in preparations for the exhibition, which was to come the evening after examination, and to consist in tableaux, plays, and music.

They did n't seem to wish us small boys to have any part in the entertainment, and Will felt rather hurt in consequence. Mr Pomeroy had requested them to enact a play entitled, "Scenes in the Life of the Hebrew Law-giver." The Hebrew law-giver was Moses. They were n't at all pleased with the play, because it was old and stupid, but they did n't dare refuse Mr. Pomeroy.

"Let me be the infant Moses," said Will.

"The idea of it!" replied Miss Belle Rhodes, who was to be Pharaoh's daughter.

"Then let me be the Hebrew who slew the Egyptian in the wilderness," said Will.

No; he could n't be that.

"Let me be the Egyptian, then."

No; they did n't want him upon the stage in any capacity, and would n't have him.

"I'll be one of the frogs that overrun the

land but that I'll go on, now," said he to me, privately.

From some remarks dropped at home, I found out that Aunt Lovisa's gentleman, Mr. Jackson, of Troas, was coming to our house about the time school closed, and though my mother has taught me never to talk of family affairs away from home, I happened to mention this piece of news to Will. He seemed to think it the best joke of the season.

"I see fun ahead, Rob," said he, "and I do hope she'll marry him; for it'll be a blessing in disguise to you, and you'll have no end of cold chicken and ice-cream at the wedding."

During the last few weeks of the term, Cynthia Strong, who is usually so pert and snappish, was extremely sober, and Home one day asked her if she was under "concern of mind." Will and I one day found out her trouble.

Mr. Strong lives a half-mile out of the village. He is town-collector, and we had been out there with money to pay our fathers' taxes, and were coming home across lots, and about crossing the brook, when we heard some one crying and sobbing behind a clump of willows. We peeped around, and there was Cynthia all in a little heap, her face hid in her lap. We were afraid she had fallen and hurt herself, and Will went up and touched her on the shoulder. She flounced up and looked at us, but did n't attempt to rise.

"Are you hurt?" asked Will.

"No; but I wish I was. I can't go anywhere, nor do anything, nor have anything like other girls; it 's nothing but trouble, trouble, *trouble!*"

"What troubles?"

"Everything."

"Well, what in particular?"

"You 'll make fun of me if I tell you; you all make fun of me, you think I 'm a great awkward, homely girl, and I am, but I can't help it. I 'd be glad to be nice and pretty as Rose Payson is, but I was n't made so well in the beginning; 't is n't my fault. I don't want to grow so fast, nor to have my hands spread and my feet bulge; but they do, and my wrists grow bony, the freckles come, and *here I be!*"

"We won't make fun of you, and you don't look so very badly, Cynthia," said Will, going down on the grass beside her.

"Yes, I do," retorted Cynthia, twisting her handkerchief hard. "I know just how I look; and examination day I've got to look — oh, I've got to look like a reg'lar little — *beggar!* That old pink delaine is all I'll have to wear, and that is streaked and spotted and faded; the skirt and the sleeves are too short; it pinches everywhere and the hooks and eyes keep bursting off, — I shall be a credit to the school, shan't I?"

Will did n't seem to know what to say.

"As long as Sue Vallandigham wore her old dress, I thought I could stand it; but her mother's bought her a beautiful blue merino, and it does seem as if I *shall die!* I wish I might, and go and be an angel, and have a robe I should n't grow out of. Oh-h dear!"

"Won't your father get you a new dress?"

"No, he can't, there are so many of us children, and we have such appetites, and he can't get pay for his last job. It's dreadful to be poor and go to school with rich girls. I've a great mind to run away."

"You'd have to go looking worse than you do now, and maybe not have enough to eat," said I, somewhat frightened.

"I know that; but the girls would n't be looking on, and I should n't be so dreadfully,— *dr-ead*-fully ashamed. Just the minute my father gives me leave, I'm going away to work; and I'll work day and night, — day and night, — and *won't* I have some clothes? I'll have a black silk dress that'll stand alone, and a blue poplin as stiff as a board, I will. They'll see then — those girls with their plaid silks and gold chains — that Cynthia Strong is as good as any of 'em, they will."

With this, Cynthia straightened up, wiped her eyes, rolled her handkerchief into a hard knot, and appeared so brave and determined that she seemed in a better mood to leave than in the weeping one. Will told her he thought it would all, in some way, come out right, and we left.

"I'm sorry for her, Bob, and she will look

like the Witch of Endor; for she did at the last examination, and she's grown ever so much since," said Will.

"Let's put our money together, and earn enough more to buy her a dress," said I. "You and I might as well be doing something as Charlie Payson."

Will approved, and that evening I asked my mother's consent. Aunt Lovisa laughed, and said Will and I had grown "very chivalric" The two wrinkles came between my mother's eyes, and said she, "I fully approve of Rob's trying to help the little girl, Lovisa."

My mother never laughs at my plans whether they're "chivalric" or not. She gave me something to do for which she said she would pay me, and Will did errands for his father. By the next Saturday night we had each earned a dollar and a quarter. We tried to interest Home in our project.

"It's one of Will's new goodish notions, is n't it?" asked he privately of me.

"I don't know what you mean by goodish notions," retorted I.

"Take that for a specimen, then. Will has been running over with them since he came under parson Edward Hammond's influence. He is ra-a-ther improving, though; he *tries* not to be so tricky —"

"Will you join us?" interrupted I.

"Don't believe I can, Rob. Much obliged for the privilege, but spending-money 's too scarce, and Cynthia too snappish. You ought n't to expect a growing boy to stand and deliver every time a girl outgrows her gown."

I wonder why, when some people are asked to do a thing just once, they always put in the "every time"! Charlie gave seventy-five cents, Ed, a dollar, and my mother and Mrs. Payson the remainder. Mr. Bradley let us have the material — blue merino like Sue's — at cost, and Mrs. Hammond hired it made, and fitted it to Mollie, who is about Cynthia's size.

When it was completed, we folded it up into a parcel, pinned on it a card inscribed, "Miss Cynthia Strong, from a few of her Friends," and put it under her desk. She came in late, and looking extremely miserable. She put her hand under the desk after her Testament, and hit the parcel; she drew it out, read the note, and looked bewildered.

All through prayers she kept taking little peeps in at one end of the parcel, and immediately afterwards she tucked it under her apron, and asked to "g' wout." When she returned her face was all aglow.

"I've heard of angels bringing folks things," said she, at noon, "but I never expected any of 'em would come near *me!*"

CHAPTER XV.

EXAMINATION AND EXHIBITION.

EXAMINATION came, as usual, on Friday. We attended morning session, but did nothing except perform a few examples, and arrange for the afternoon. A dread was on us as if a great crisis was at hand.

When we met in the afternoon we had on our best clothes, and, in some way, it seemed as if we must get acquainted over again. Will had on a new pair of boots that squeaked outrageously.

We were to sit three at a desk, so as to make room for the spectators, and we had to put a board across the two chairs at each desk, in order to make room for the third scholar. Our board was rather too short, and there was danger of its slipping off at one end. Tommy Taylor sat with us, and Will gave him a charge before school commenced.

"Now, Tommy," said he, "you'll have to sit still and think of solemn things, because if you get uneasy, and begin cutting up any didos, this board'll slip, and you'll go down, slam bang."

Tommy solemnly promised that he would n't move, folded his arms, and sat up stiff and still as a statue.

The first class called was our grammar class.

Homer usually sits first on the recitation seat, and he had been all the morning studying up the first questions, and preparing to show off; but when the class was called, what should Cynthia Strong do but establish herself on that end seat! Home motioned and motioned to her to move along; but she would n't budge an inch, and poor Home had to take his place second.

Cynthia recited through all the first part, and then Home was called up. He had on an upright pointed collar, that stuck into his throat, and made him look as if choking, while his green necktie gave him a jaundice-y appearance.

"Homer, what is a noun?" asked the master.

"A noun —" gasped Homer; "a noun is — a noun shows whether it's first, second, or third persons."

"What are the properties of nouns, Homer?"

"The properties of nouns —" said Homer, "are three: masculine, feminine, common, and neuter."

"What do you mean by the number of a noun?"

"The number of a noun shows how many parts it's divided into, whether first, second, or third."

"That'll do," said the master.

Homer sat down, looking as if he'd done credit to his instructions, however it might be with the remainder of the class.

Will came next, and the master began putting the same questions to him. He immediately took the subject of nouns into his own hands, as if a noun was a kind of toy with which he was perfectly familiar; told all he knew and more too, and wound up with the declension of a noun in a full, clear voice.

The spectators exchanged approving glances.

Will is a wonderful boy for examinations. He don't have remarkable lessons during term time; but when examination comes, the excitement of having visitors in school just fires him up, and everything he ever studied, read, or heard, comes to him. Company affects me and most of the other boys in a different way, and we forget everything we ever knew.

By the time our geography was called, the room was full of visitors. Oh, how I did wish I was one of them! Will, who is always very polite on such occasions, carried his geography to the committee, and his boots went squeak, squeak, *squeak*, all the way out. Mr. Pomeroy shook his head as if his geographical information had been called in question, and Will squeaked back again.

The master first examined us on Europe. Then Mr. Pomeroy began with his questions.

"For what is Vienna noted?"

"For the lovely palace of Schonbrunn," replied Will.

"For being situated on a great number of small islands," corrected Mr. Pomeroy.

"Are n't you thinking of Venice, sir?" asked Will, respectfully.

Mr. Pomeroy acknowledged that he was thinking of Venice, and Will got credit for knowing more than the committee.

When we came on to Africa, Will bounded Soudan, and named its provinces with great accuracy and distinctness.

"Now bound the State of New York," said Mr. Royce.

"We don't take York State this term, sir," said Cynthia.

Will blundered through the boundary, though, and Mr. Royce smiled, and said we'd better perfectly understand the geography of our own country before we went on to Soudan. Thereupon Will woke up, and bounded the state over again, mentioned the lakes, rivers, and mountains, named and located the principal towns, gave heights, lengths, and breadths, and went into details generally with an ease and a fluency that brought down the house, and astonished no one, I think, so much as himself. Mr. Royce joined in the applause.

We went on to Oceanica, and Homer told how the natives of the Friendly Isles killed and ate Captain Cook. That 's Home's standard item on Oceanica. He may forget everything else, but he never forgets that the natives of the Friendly Isles killed and ate Captain Cook.

When our arithmetic was called, Will looked and acted as if he could recite right through the book, from numeration to mensuration, without pausing. To have heard him reel off the rule for partial payments, one would n't have suspected but that he could perform the examples as easily as any in simple addition.

Mr. Royce questioned us on interest, Mr. Pomeroy on fractions. Fractions are Mr. Pomeroy's hobby. We finished them, and were examined on them last term, but they had to be raked up again. He said he would ask a few practical questions, and after he was through with his practical questions, he said he would like to have William Bradley write a few decimals on the board.

"You may write," said he, "one million one hundred thousand and one; one million, one hundred thousand, one hundred and one trillionths."

Will was standing by me, and he fairly groaned out at that. He 's always in a muddle about writing decimals, and for my part, I don't know who is n't. He dashed down ones and ciphers, and when he had quite a string of them, began rubbing out some, and putting in others, affixing, prefixing, and fixing in the middle until it was in a general jumble. Finally he made a dab with the chalk for a decimal point, and began reading.

Mr. Pomeroy, who, through his glasses, had overlooked all operations, said he was n't reading it aright, and if he did read it right, 't was n't what he was told to set down. Then Mr. Pomeroy tried to read what was on the board, and to tell what ought to be there, and to help fix it. Will maintained that what he gave out now was n't what he gave out the first time, and they both grew confused. They could n't agree on what the original number was, nor on what they had written, nor on what they wanted to write, and they grew more and more confused, and neither of them knew what the other was talking about, nor what he himself was talking about. Mr. Pomeroy had grown red in the face, Will had come to that point where, according to 'Bijah Whittlesey, "he 's as sot as a mule"; and there 's no knowing what they would have come to, had n't the master interposed.

"It 's some time since the boy studied decimals. Perhaps I 'd better give him a problem elsewhere," said he, in his blandest tones.

Mr. Pomeroy straightened himself up, and said perhaps the boy *had* better have a problem elsewhere; he *was* rather bewildered; and, between them both, they set "the boy" at work.

Then came Tommy Taylor to the board. (He is n't in our class, but this day he was reciting with us.) He took his place between Will and I, and gave a sympathetic grin to each of us. As soon as he had read over his example, he ran up his hand, and said he, —

"This ain't the example I did this morning."

Will snatched his hand down.

"Don't you know *beans*, Tommy?" whispered he.

But Tommy will do just as he 's a mind to. He twitched away his hand, and hoisted it up again.

"Please, sir," drawled he, "this ain't my example."

"Perform the example that 's assigned you, or else take your seat," retorted the master, flushing up.

After this recitation we had nothing more to do except listen to the large scholars. Sue Vallandigham got so uneasy, she began writing, tipped the ink over on her white apron, and had to "g 'wout" in a state of great agitation.

Just after the scholarship reports were read, a dead silence fell in the room, and Ed Hammond stepped forward and presented the master with our "testimonial of affectionate esteem." This year our "testimonial" was a beautifully finished angler's rod, and a case containing all varieties and sizes of what Home called "trout and sucker tools." Ed made an excellent speech that set everybody laughing, the master made a funny reply, and the solemn awfulness of examination day was a good deal broken up.

Nothing then remained but the remarks. How I do hate the remarks!

Tommy Taylor grew restless, and began fidgeting in a way that was dangerous. Will tried to stop him, but he would keep wriggling and twisting.

"Tommy," whispered Will, at last, "I've a big fish-hook—a pickerel hook—in my pocket, and if you don't sit stiller, I'll hook it into you and hold you still."

Upon that Tommy quieted down a little.

Mr. Pomeroy made the closing remarks, and addressed himself particularly to the large boys and girls who were not to return. He was at the most pathetic point, and the girls were weeping, when Tommy gave a most agonizing wriggle, his board slipped, and down he went with a crash. He struck against the iron standard of the desk, cut his lips, and set up a howl. When he saw the blood running he thought he was killed, and screamed worse than ever. Will clapped his hand over his mouth, and dragged him out. That little accident interrupted the flow of speech-making, and we were soon dismissed.

In the evening, we had in the hall a very good exhibition of tableaux and dialogues. Once in a while, we small boys were brought on the stage to fill up a background, but most of the time we were employed in carrying messages between the boys' and the girls' dressing-rooms or in running on errands outside.

The dressing-rooms were small, the actors numerous, and things much mixed. Two fairies had a bitter quarrel about their wands. The beautiful princess had the headache, and was smelling camphor, and the poor but honest youth who was to win her said he'd be hanged if he'd brought his handkerchief. Louis XVI appropriated the costume of Napoleon Bonaparte, Marie Antoinette could n't find her pearl necklace, and the Empress Josephine set up a weeping and a wailing, because some one had tipped a bottle of perfumery on her lavender silk robe.

Will and I were despatched to the nearest

neighbor's to dry the lavender robe, and when we returned there was no one in the boys' dressing-room but Home. He said the other boys were either on the stage or among the audience. He appeared flurried, and his breath smelled of medicine.

Will began clearing out a chair to sit down upon. He gave a toss to an old revolver of Napoleon Bonaparte's, and it fell on the table, shivering a small hand-mirror of Harry Blakeslee's.

"Jerusalem!" ejaculated Will.

"There's a dollar and a half out of your pocket," said Home, composedly.

"Just my luck," replied Will, as he picked up the broken glass. "So surely as I get my debts paid up, and a little something ahead, so that I can begin to enjoy life, I smash up something or other, and have to rake and scrape, plan and pinch, to pay damages."

"Look here, Will," said Home, glancing around him, and speaking low, "leave the pistol as it fell, and we'll go out among the audience. In a minute or two there'll be a dozen or more boys in here turning things over and throwing them around, and by the time Harry finds his glass broken, he 'll be as likely to suspect some one else as you."

Will faced around upon Home.

"I wonder, Homer Sharpe," said he, "if you think I 'd do that thing! You have a high opinion of me, have n't you? You think I'm a brave sort of a boy, don't you?"

Will looked so angry and excited I was afraid we were going to have a quarrel, but just then the boys from the stage came crowding in.

"Harry," said Will, as soon as he had an opportunity, "I 've done something you will think ought to send me to the reform school."

"Don't doubt it," said Harry, turning over a pile of clothes in the corner.

Will explained, and Harry took it quite coolly. We were both much relieved, for Harry is n't always sweet-tempered, and we had expected he would storm.

Another scene on the stage was soon arranged, and the dressing-room was thinned out.

"I should like to know," said Gustus Hillman, who had remained, "what has become of my troches. I left a full box on the table, and there are n't half a dozen here now."

I remembered just then how Home's breath had smelled. He was now holding a big cologne bottle to his nose, and did n't appear to hear a word of what was being said.

"Well," said Ike, giving Gustus a wink, "if anybody has eaten all those troches, he 's a dead man!"

Homer dropped the cologne-bottle stopper he had begun licking.

"Oh-h!" exclaimed Gustus, greatly distressed, "I hope no one has eaten them. One is a dose for a full-grown man!"

"Even now," said Ike, gravely, "the poor wretch may be quietly sitting among the audienee. If he could but be warned in season to take the antidote —"

"What is the antidote?" gasped Home.

"Oil," replied Ike, quickly; "oil, promptly administered, and in a dose sufficiently large to prevent the troches eating through the *epigistratrum* into the *pericardium*."

Homer turned ashy white, and clawed at the pit of his stomach.

"They 've begun eating a'ready," groaned he.

"Have you eaten those troches?" demanded Ike, seizing Home by the shoulder. "Tell me, Homer Sharpe, have you eaten those troches?"

Home tremblingly acknowledged that he had.

"And they were the real bronchial troches, made out of the strongest kind of *bronchia!* Tell me quick, Home, do you feel any irritation of the æsophagus or oscillation of the epiglottis?"

"Yes, yes," groaned Home, "the pepper-glottis is bad — they 've begun eating — I feel 'em. Has n't anybody any oil, — not any kind of oil?"

"Kerosene?" said Ike, looking at Gustus.

Gustus shook his head at Ike.

"There 's a bottle of what druggists call 'bear's grease' at the bottom of my trunk, over there. You get that out, Ike, while I rub him."

"Do you think he 'll die, Will?" asked I.

"Just you hold on for a while, Bob. Home is always eating things and meddling with what don't belong to him. Let the boys manage him."

"Now, Home," said Gustus, taking the cork out of the bottle, "this is a hair-dressing abomination I've had two years, and the druggist had a year before me. It won't be very pleasant to take."

Home said he did n't care for that; he could stand anything but this *gnawing*. He took the bottle, and had swallowed one half its contents, when Gustus snatched it away.

"Don't let us kill you, Home," said he.

"Are you sure I've taken enough?" asked Home, with tears in his eyes.

A regretful look came over Gustus's face, and he did n't reply; but Ike answered briskly that the oil was sure to soften and neutralize the effect of the troches, and that, being bear's oil, it was peculiarly calculated to counteract the gnawing. He hustled Home on to a trunk, and ordered him to lie flat on his back, while he piled on overcoats enough to induce perspiration.

The little room was close and hot, and by the time the boys came in from the stage, Home was in a pretty moist condition, and groaning with nausea. Ike explained his condition, and Ed Hammond turned on his heels and walked away; but the other boys questioned Home in regard to his feelings, and suggested things he had better take. Home answered them in a faint voice, and lay with his eyes closed. He said the gnawing had ceased, but he had a deathly kind of feeling inside.

"Of course," said Ike, "it's the troches dying off from the effects of the oil."

Ike had to go on the stage in the next tableau, and before going he pronounced Home out of danger.

Home crawled out into the audience-room, and lounged on the end of a settee, where, later in the evening, I saw him trading off slate pencils for sassafras lozenges.

Soon came on the play, "Scenes in the Life of the Hebrew Law-giver."

Belle had fixed upon little Willie Tucker, Ike's cousin, for the Moses; but, before the play came on, Willie was fast asleep on a pile of clothes in our dressing-room.

"Don't you wake him up. You let me be the infant Moses," said Will privately to Ike.

Only a few evenings before, Ike had been badly snubbed by Miss Belle. Here he had an opportunity for revenge, and on Will's urging the matter, he consented.

"The white dress that large-sized fairy, Susannah Vallandigham, wore will fit me; and you can fix on Willie Tucker's pink sash and shoulder knots to make me look pretty," said Will.

I was sent to borrow the dress, and having an unusually amiable freak, Sue gave it to me without a question. We dressed Will down in the basement where it was cold as Greenland, but where none of the boys could see us.

Then Ike wrapped him up in a shawl, and together we carried him on the stage and laid him in the clothes-basket among the cat's-tail reeds that represented bulrushes. Pharaoh's daughter and maidens were so absorbed in arraying themselves that they didn't look after the Moses.

Belle inquired of Ike if Willie was ready. Ike replied that Will was ready, and the curtain was rung up.

Pharaoh's daughter and her maidens, looking very beautiful, came slowly down to the river's bank. Pharaoh's daughter, in a very sweet voice, was giving advice to her maidens. Soon a cry was heard from amid the bulrushes.

"List!" said Pharaoh's daughter, raising her forefinger. "I hear an infant's wail."

The train of maidens paused and listed.

"*Ya, ya, ya!*" went Will from among the reeds.

"The sound, methinks, proceeds from yonder tiny boat amid the reeds. Advance, and discover to me what it may be. Perchance the offspring of some fond Israelitish mother may be saved from the cruel edict of my father."

Almina Harris, who was Maid No. 1, advanced towards the basket. Almina had been selected as Maid No. 1, because she was strong enough in the arms to bring forward the infant.

"It is a Hebrew child, my lady; one of the accursed race which thy father seeks to destroy," said she, drawing the mosquito net off the child's face.

"Bring him hither! I would myself behold

the innocent, unjustly doomed to be cut off in the morning of his existence."

Almina was too stupefied by what she had found, to reply. Will straddled out of the basket, knocked over a good many "cat-tails," and came tramping up to Pharaoh's daughter.

"Here I be," said he.

There he stood, smiling tranquilly, while Pharaoh's daughter was aghast.

Stillness reigned for an instant, and then the audience burst into laughter. The maidens ran off the stage, and on Pharaoh's daughter and the infant Moses facing each other, the curtain fell with a crash.

By the time Ike and I got behind the scenes again, the excitement was tremendous. Pharaoh's daughter was in hysterics, and the maidens wanted Pharaoh to execute the infant Moses without further delay. When we appeared, a general attack was made upon Ike, and Harry Blakeslee, who was Pharaoh, was disposed to execute him along with the infant.

Ike coolly put on his hat, and said he thought he would step out and take the air. Will and I, having returned the white dress to the enraged and sputtering Susanna, followed him.

The remaining scenes in the "Life of the Hebrew Law-giver," were dispensed with. The remaining plays and tableaux passed off without anything particularly interesting occurring behind the scenes.

The large scholars, many of whom are n't coming back another term, remained after the audience had dispersed, to hold a farewell interview. Will and I remained to see what it consisted in. It was pretty much all weeping and kissing. They tried to sing "Auld Lang Syne," but broke down on it, and had more kissing and weeping, bade each other good-by, and started home in companies that soon paired off. Will and I made one pair.

CHAPTER XVI.

CONCLUSION BY ORDER OF AUNT LOVISA.

SATURDAY morning Aunt Lovisa was expecting Mr. Jackson, and there was so much sweeping, dusting, and getting ready at our house that I could n't stand it, and went down to Mr. Bradley's store for comfort. Will was sitting on the counter swinging his legs and holding a political discussion with Capt. Parker.

"If Lincoln is elected and slavery allowed in the territories, the South will secede, and this glorious Union will be disrupted! Hallo, Bob," said he patronizingly, looking down upon me.

I sprang up beside him and told him of the state of affairs at our house. Just then the train came in, and pretty soon we saw a tall man with a portmanteau pass the door.

"That 's the man," said I.

"O Jerusalem!" said Will, "if I was a woman, I would as soon be courted by a broomstick."

"I like to have him at our house," said I, "for we always have three kinds of cake for tea, and Aunt Lovisa passes the basket to me every time. Usually she thinks rich cake is bad for a boy."

"Let's go see the meeting," said Will.

We ran, but we did n't reach the house until Aunt Lovisa had taken him into the parlor. All that we in the hall could hear was a murmur of voices.

Will put on the shiny hat, and, with Mr. Jackson's cane, walked up and down the hall in Mr. Jackson's stiff gait, and saluted me as Aunt Lovisa. We had all the fun we could, and it was all the more fun because we knew Aunt Lovisa had sharp ears, and a loud titter would bring her out.

"I wonder if this is a present," whispered Will, taking up a brown-paper package that seemed to hold a box. "Oh! I know what I'll do," said he, pulling out his pill-box of sneezing snuff. I don't suppose there's been a time since

Will came out of "knickerbockers" but he 's carried sneezing snuff in his pocket. He rubbed the powder on both sides the package.

Just then we heard steps approaching the parlor door, and we dodged into the closet under the stairs. The hat Will wore struck against the upper casement of the low door and rolled off. We had barely time to get it in with us when out came Mr. Jackson. As he went to the table for his package he brushed past the closet, and the door shut with a snap, and that door don't open on the inside. I did n't think of it then, though, for I was as excited as Will was, anticipating fun with the snuff.

Mr. Jackson went back to the parlor, and Will set me off into giggles by saying, "Now — now — going to begin, Bob! Now!"

When it did begin I thought I should have died. First came Aunt Lovisa with little cat sneezes, a dozen at a time; then Mr. Jackson, in great horse sneezes that seemed to shake the house; then both together. We heard them flying around, opening windows and doors, and

Will said he hoped they'd both lost their handkerchiefs.

"Why, why (sneeze), I (sneeze) don't understand (sneeze, sneeze) what it means (sneeze, sneeze, *sneeze*)," went Mr. Jackson.

"*Cayenne!*" gasped Aunt Lovisa, with a dozen small sneezes.

Then they both went off in a chorus.

Will laughed till he tipped over, and he tipped on to Mr. Jackson's hat. That frightened us, and still we kept on tittering. There seemed to be all the coal-hods and dust brushes and pans in the house in that closet, and we kept hitting things and knocking things down and tumbling into things..

Finally the commotion in the parlor subsided, and we began to think about ourselves. Will tried opening the door-spring with a stove poker, but could n't. We put our shoulders against the door and pushed with all our might, and Will tried to encourage me by whispering, "Now, now! There she goes! Give us liberty or give us death!"

But she did n't "go," and it began to look as

if we should have death for all of liberty. I sat down in a coal-hod to take breath, and Will on a cricket. The cricket was an infirm one, its four legs spread out like a spider's, and down he went. For a half-minute he sat reflecting.

"Do let's scream," said I.

"No, I won't scream. Let's give her one more push," said he.

We braced our backs against the side of the narrow closet, put our feet against the door, and pushed with all our might. The spring gave way, the door flew back against the wall, we boys went down among the iron and tin ware, and out came Aunt Lovisa.

"Ah! it's *you*, is it, William Bradley?" said she, as if light was breaking in upon her. "You're the worst boy in town; and I do think Almira is just insane to allow Rob to associate with you!"

Will brushed himself, swung the door together so as to hide the hat, and walked off. As soon as Aunt Lovisa returned to the parlor, we slipped back, took the hat, and carried it up to mother. Will confessed the whole affair to her.

"Why, Willy, how could you?" said she. "It was very naughty. I can't allow such practical jokes in my house; I really can't."

She was, at first, a good deal frightened about the hat, but she pressed, and smoothed, and brushed, until it looked as well as ever, and she herself carried it back and hung it on the rack, and Will went home.

After tea I went down to Will's and found him lying on the grass looking very dejected. He said Ed Hammond had been reproving him for playing off such jokes as he had at the exhibition.

"And such as I 've been at again to-day," said he.

"Then Ed is a prig," said I.

"No, he is n't, Rob; he only let me know, in that way he has of saying little and meaning much, what he thought of certain performances, and he 's right, Rob. I honor 'Bijah Whittlesey and your aunt for their opinions of me."

Just then up came Ed balancing the schoolhouse key on his finger. He was going after his books.

"I 'm sorry I gave you pain, Will," said he, "but I do despise small-boy tricks. I want you to try to overcome your propensity for them. Fun, like everything else, has its metes and bounds. You 're one of the kind who need to think twice before they act. Come over to the school-house now. We 're friends, are n't we?"

Ed reached down his hand and Will grasped it and rose by it, and we went on to the school-house. The sun was shining in full at the west windows, but the great school-room looked lonely. Ed walked around tapping the desks thoughtfully, and a fly buzzed through the empty room.

"Boys," said Ed at length, "it will be but a little while before you, too, will be leaving the old school-room. It looks a long way ahead, I know, but you won't find it so, and you 'll feel badly at the last,—you can't help it; and you 'll be full of regrets just in proportion as you 've neglected those little opportunities for showing kindnesses that are always coming up in school, and that, once let slip, never return. Now, boys, if you want your school-days pleasant in the retrospect, you must help each other."

"Well, Ed dear, we do mean to, but you see we don't *think*."

"Oh! I know that, but we *ought* to think, and I do believe we may be helped to remember these things. I want to make my experience of some use to you, and I am going to give you a little summary of advice.

"Help one another. Hold to the right side, be it never so unpopular; hold firmly and come out strongly just in proportion as you feel it is right. Don't tease the girls, nor fret the master, nor shirk your lessons. Despise sly, tricky ways. If you 've something that you feel you must do or die, do it openly and take your penalty like men."

"Amen!" ejaculated Will. "We 'll try, and you can once in a while write to us from your college off there, and reinforce your admonitions by gentle suggestions."

We walked around the room arm-in-arm a little while; then Ed took out his books and strapped them up, and we went out. In the hall he stood with his hand on the door-knob, and took a long survey of the room.

"O Ed!" exclaimed I, "we've only just found out what a good friend you are, and now you're never, *never* coming here to school any more!"

I could n't keep back the tears. Ed laughed, pulled out his handkerchief, and gave a brush first at my eyes and then his own.

"Don't let 's have a farewell scene this evening," said Will. "We'll see you again, Ed. Come on, Bob."

We nodded good-evening and ran for home.

. . . .

MONDAY MORNING.

Mr. Jackson has gone, and Aunt Lovisa is — "tired and nervous," mother says. She has been reading over this writing of mine, and she says it's very silly and has been a great waste of time.

"Besides, Almira," said she, "he's been using up this sermon-paper his Uncle Robert bought before he went off to California to die. It's perfect sacrilege!"

With that she took out what little paper was left in the lower drawer, and went off with it. I can write no more.

CHAPTER XVII.

HOW WE TURN OUT.

BAYWATER, SEPTEMBER, 1876.

YESTERDAY mother was up garret, rummaging chests, overturning barrels, getting stung by wasps, and having dreadful times generally, and I had reached the foot of the stairs with spirits of ammonia for the stings, when a manuscript book of yellow sermon-paper came fluttering down at my feet.

"There 's that kind of a chronicle you kept when you were a little boy, Rob. I should think you would wish to preserve it," called mother.

I set the ammonia down on the stairs, and retired to examine the book. I 've concluded to revise it, add a chapter, and petition a friend of my father's, who owns an interest in a publishing house, to give it to the public.

I see that it closed with Aunt Lovisa. It

may as well resume with Aunt Lovisa. She was married the Thanksgiving after my chronicle closes, and we not only had ice-cream and cold chicken in abundance, but I was allowed to invite in my friends, Charles, William, and Homer, and, to quote from the latter classic, "We had a bully time of it."

Aunt Lovisa went to Troas to live, and as soon as I realized that she had left us forever, I began to suffer the pangs of remorse.

Not a repentant word that I uttered, not a tear-drop that I let fall, did my mother fail to transmit a record of to Aunt Lovisa. In course of time there came to me a letter proffering my aunt's full and free forgiveness, and, what seemed quite as much to the point, enclosing a dollar bill. An intimation was, to be sure, conveyed that the donor preferred I should purchase some good and instructive book, rather than spend the money for anything "to eat"; but with the advice of my friend William, I broke the bill into cocoanut and taffy drops.

Aunt Lovisa has now two boys of her own, and if Will and I were ever such aggressive, intractable, exasperating little wretches as these are, I can't blame my aunt for having wanted mercy towards us heavily laden with justice. The last time they were at our house, the youngest screamed himself purple in the face after cake.

"People don't know *any*thing what it is to bring up a child until they 've tried it for themselves," said Aunt Lovisa.

Upon that she cuddled him up to her, and began feeding him preserves.

Will is now in Boston, in the employ of his uncle, a prominent wholesale dry-goods dealer, and a childless man. He has the prospect of one day being received as a partner in the firm. I am still plodding away with my father in the Baywater bank. The first of next November I am to have a good place in the Sidon N. Y. Second National.

Perhaps I can't better give an idea of the present status, absolute and relative, of us Baywater boys, than by giving an account of my last Spring's visit to Will.

While I was waiting at the Baywater depot

on that occasion, in came Charlie Payson, bound west.

Charlie is one of the finest looking young men that ever came up in these parts, and has that indescribable but never-to-be-mistaken air which distinguishes a *man* from those dependent, drifting, going-to-the dogs class of fellows one meets at every turn. He had come from Chicago only the day before.

"You make a short visit," said I.

"Yes; but I can't extend it. In fact, I ought not to have come at all, but mother and Rose start on their European trip next week, and I felt as if I must just run home and say good-by."

"You are getting to be the Western man of business, always pressed for time, are you, then?"

"Yes, I am, Rob. I 've got a good start for a youngster, but if a young man is going to make any place for himself in the world, with all this rush and competition on all sides of him, he can't very often let up for a play-day."

"The old wheelbarrow, Payson's Express, and

the black horse have retired from active service, I suppose."

"Yes. I've more regard for that old wheel-barrow, though, than for any other piece of inanimate matter between the two oceans. If ever I get to be a prominent business man, I'll trundle it out and I'll say to the boys, 'There, young men; there's the foundation of my success in life!' You see, Rob, I stuck to that thing night and morning, day in and day out, until I earned enough to buy the old horse and wagon. After that I laid up money, and when I started for Chicago the day I was twenty-one, I took with me a capital that I would n't have exchanged for a gift of thousands from my father. There are some things worth more to a young man starting in business than money, you know that, Rob."

I said something about his father's abundant resources.

"Father has over and over again offered to help me, but I don't want it. If I can't walk, I'll squat; but I won't go hobbling along on borrowed crutches. No, sir; when I deliver my grand wheelbarrow lecture, I shall say, 'Learn first to use your own legs, boys, and then stand on them; don't be asking the loan of some one else's.'"

"Gustus Hillman is in Chicago, is n't he?" asked I.

"Yes; Gustus has worked his way up from a local reporter's place to a sub-editorship on the 'Trumpet,' and he has an outlook on something higher. He has every now and then a turn of despondency when no one's trials and discouragements are like his own; but he has the good sense never to write his articles in blue ink. When he comes out of the depths, he 's in fine feather, and is wonderfully popular with his professional brethren."

The down-train whistled just then and we took leave of each other.

It rained a little that morning, and about twenty-five miles this side of Boston there entered the car a female figure, heavily draped with damp water-proof cloth and enveloped about the head with blue berege. She seated herself by me, and as she removed her veil, whisked the water-drops in my face. I recognized an old acquaintance.

"Miss Vallandigham," said I.

"Mr. Brown," responded she.

It was Sue. She had become a temperance lecturess, and I was interested in getting her report of herself. She said she had been lecturing three seasons, ever since the family left Baywater; that she drew respectably sized houses, and her receipts paid her expenses and left her fair wages, nothing more.

I felt sorry for her. She had lectured the previous evening, and had an engagement for the coming evening, and she looked disheartened and seemed to be in a peculiarly limp, starchless condition. It must be discouraging, — trying to reform mankind in the bulk, when so many of her sex lamentably fail with the individual specimen.

At a smoky little station she left to take the stage, and as I saw her steaming water-proof shut into the crowded vehicle, I wished in my heart, for the hundredth time, that so many human beings did n't make mistakes in finding out for what they 're fitted in life.

I had a number of errands to discharge in Boston, and did n't get around to Will's quarters until nearly dark. I found him quite luxuriously established. His parlor was large and fine, and had a wonderfully home-like, social look, — books and pictures, a piano and violin, statuary, plants in the windows, and all that sort of thing, I must have betrayed my surprise, for after a while Will said, "This establishment is uncle's. Aunt comes down with a servant once or twice a week, and gives it those little feminine touches we read so much about, but which janitors and chambermaids, in some way, never seem to get the knack of. You 'll by and by see to what use we put it."

Before lighting up the room, Will put fresh coal on his fire, and we sat down for a talk. Will told me how fortunate he had been in pleasing his uncle, and how he had every year laid up a part of his salary. I told him how I came to obtain the place in Sidon, what salary

I was to have, where I was to board, when I was going to take Nellie Royce there, and all that sort of thing. I gave him the Baywater news and all the personal gossip of the town.

"Home and Cynthia continue to live harmoniously, do they?" asked he.

"Oh, beautifully! Home runs the tin-shop, as did his father, while Cynthia's dress-making and millinery establishment eclipses anything outside the cities."

"Home sent me an invitation to the wedding," said Will. "I had n't seen Cynthia for some time, and when she swept into church in her white silk and laces, I never was so completely astonished in my life. She was fairly queenly! And there was Home, standing at least three inches higher in his boots than usual, and looking as if he thought every man in the church was dying with envy. And to think of the way he and I used to tease that girl—'t was too funny!"

"I sometimes contrast her executive abilities with those of some men of her years,—Tommy Taylor's, for instance," said I.

"That reminds me of something I never told you. At the time of my last and only visit to the Baywater High School, four or five years ago, Tommy was in the upper class, and had that day taken his first lesson in Virgil. He read, —

"'*Arma virumque cano, Trojæ,' etc.*

"Then soberly and seriously translated it, —

"'A man took a dog in his arms and went to Troy.'"

"That's a fair sample of Tommy. He went to San Francisco a month or two ago, to take a situation an uncle had offered him, and he bought a ticket for the Isthmus route, because his uncle fifteen years ago went by the Isthmus route. If San Francisco don't give some of his ideas a shaking up I shall be very much surprised."

"The most comfort-taking man in Baywater," said I, "is Ike Tucker. He is head machinist in one of the shops, has run two or three patents through the office, and succeeded in obtaining as much for them as he expended. He married Almina Harris, you know."

"And of his two sons, one is named Isaac Edward, and one Gustus William," said Will.

"I went to see Ed Hammond last fall," continned Will. "I owe a great deal to Ed, and he's grand, Rob! he's a man to measure by. He's down there on the Maine coast with a large congregation of sailors, fishermen, and lumbermen, — as rough a looking set as ever you saw. He went at first as missionary or something of that sort, with no idea of staying, but he fairly built up a church there, and now I suppose he could n't be induced to leave. In the warm season the city visitors in that vicinity come in to hear him, and a few months ago he received an offer of a larger salary, — a call to a wider sphere of usefulness, I mean, in a Portland church, wealthy, cultivated, fashionable audience, and all that, but he declined; said he did n't know but souls on the coast were worth as much as souls in the city. That's Ed all throngh."

Steps were heard on the stairs, and Will sprang up and lighted the gas. In a minute a couple of young men entered, and these were soon followed by four or five others. They appeared to be expected, and Will immediately entered upon their entertainment, rather they entertained themselves. Conversation, reading, and music followed each other naturally. Later in the evening, more mental exhilaration appeared than I ever before saw where I was sure there had been no artificial stimulus. When the party took leave, one of the number invited the others around to his quarters for the next evening. Will let them into the street.

"Have n't we had a good time?" asked he, as he came back. "Auntie is all the time cudgelling her brains for philanthropic schemes, and within a year or two she's been studying up on 'Duties of Employers to Their Employees.' She invites all the subordinates connected with the store to tea two or three times a year; but that she thinks don't amount to much, and she has taken up the idea of furnishing a pleasant parlor, which is open to all, and over which I am to preside. So far it has worked well. Some of the boys come in every few evenings. Sometimes auntie sends down refreshments or comes down with two or three young lady friends, musical perhaps. Our entertainments are varied as the times,— reading, music, informal discussions, burlesques of operatic and oratorical performances, anything that comes up. We have a general aim to gather improvement with our amusement, and to cultivate a kind of fraternal interest in each other."

Will then began telling me of his experiences in the city, and giving sketches and incidents, through which I saw that all his old spirit and enthusiasm, though directed in different channels from that in his boyish days, had not abated one whit.

Sunday I went to church with Will in the morning and out to his mission class in the afternoon, and we had a long visit in the evening sitting by the open coal fire in his room, Will, through all, bright and original as ever. He wound up saying, "After all, Rob, I more and more strongly feel that whatever the incidents and accidents of our lives may be, only as they strengthen our feet in the path of Duty and lead us into communion with the Right, are they valuable."

"Amen!" responded I.

[illegible]

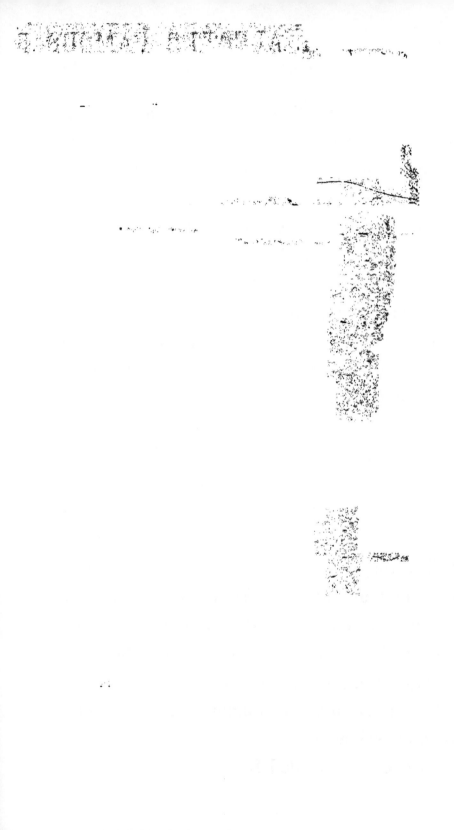

LOUISA M. ALCOTT'S FAMOUS BOOK

Jo in a Vortex. — Every few weeks she would shut herself up in her room, put on her scribbling suit, and "fall

LITTLE WOMEN: or Meg, Jo, Beth, and Amy. Par

"'I'm not hurt, all right in a minute,' he said, sitting up, a little pale and dizzy, as the boys gathered round him, full of admiration and alarm." — Page 251.

ITTLE MEN; or, Life at Plumfield with Jo's Boys. Price, $1.50.

ROBERTS BROTHERS, *Publishers, Boston.*

LOUISA M. ALCOTT'S FAMOUS BOOKS.

LOUISA M. ALCOTT'S FAMOUS BO

EIGHT COUSINS; or, T   Aunt-Hill. With Il

USAN COOLIDGE'S POPULAR BOOKS.

eat

"Now, Katy, do, — ah, do, do." — PAGE 108.

WHAT KATY DID AT SCHOOL.

WITH ILLUSTRATIONS BY MARY A. HALLOCK.

One handsome square 16mo volume, bound in cloth, black and gilt lettered. Price, $1.50.

ROBERTS BROTHERS, PUBLISHERS, BOSTON.

HOSPITAL SKETCHES. Price, $1.50.

ROBERTS BROTHERS, *Publishers*, Bo

"Sing, Tessa; sing!" cried Tommo, twanging away with all his might. —PAGE 47.

AUNT JO'S SCRAP-BAG: Containing "My Boys," "Shawl-Straps," "Cupid and Chow-Chow." 3 vols. Price of each, $1.00.

ROBERTS BROTHERS, PUBLISHERS,

Boston.

Lightning Source UK Ltd.
Milton Keynes UK
UKHW021150170119
335636UK00006B/200/P

9 780483 548077